Invasion of the Overworld:
A Minecraft novel

Mark Cheverton

Copyright 2013

Technical consultant
Gameknight999

"What we do for ourselves dies with us. What we do for others and the world remains immortal."

- Albert Pine

WHAT IS MINECRAFT?

Minecraft is a sandbox game that gives the user the ability to build amazing structures out of textured cubes, with various materials to choose from, stone, dirt, sand, sandstone, . . . Normal rules of physics don't apply, as it's possible to build structures in creative mode that defy gravity or have no visible means of support.

The creative opportunity that this program offers to users is incredible, with people building entire cities, cliff hanging civilizations, and even cities in the clouds, however the real game is not played in creative mode, it's played in survival mode. In this setting, the user is dropped into a blocky world with nothing but the clothes on their backs. Knowing that night is fast approaching, the user must gather resources, wood, stone, iron, . . . in order to craft tools and weapons, so that they can protect themselves when the monsters come; night time is monster time.

To find resources, the player must create mines, digging deep into the flesh of Minecraft in hopes of finding coal and iron, necessities in order to make metal weapons and armor, essential to survival. As they dig, the user will encounter caverns, lava filled chambers, and possibly the rare abandoned mine or dungeon, where treasures wait to be discovered, but with passageways and chambers patrolled by monsters (zombies, skeletons, and spiders) waiting to snare the unwary.

Though the land is filled with monsters, the user is not alone. Vast servers exist where hundreds of users play the game, all sharing space and resources, though they are not the only creatures in Minecraft. Villages dot the surface of the game, with NPCs (non-player characters) populating these small cities, the villagers scurrying about the village doing whatever villagers do, with chests of treasure, sometimes great, sometimes insignificant, hidden within the dwellings. By communicating with these NPCs, it's possible for users to trade items to get rare gems or materials for potions, as well as getting the occasional bow or sword.

This game is an incredible platform for people to design machines (powered by redstone, much like electrical circuits), unique games, custom maps, and PvP (player vs. player) arenas. Minecraft is a game filled with exciting creativity, spine tingling battles, and terrifying creatures. It's a rollercoaster ride through a land of adventure and suspense, with uplifting victories and bitter defeats; enjoy the ride.

CHAPTER 1 – Gameknight's game

The gigantic spider approached his hiding place slowly, methodically, its multiple red eyes burning like angry coals at the heart of a smoldering fire. Gameknight999 knew it was coming, but was not afraid. In fact, he wanted to spider to come closer, hoping he had the timing just right. Clicking sounds from the spider floated through the forest trees and reached his ears, getting louder as it neared, then more sounds from its companion; two spiders now tracking him. Leaning out to look around the trunk of the gnarled tree, he shot a quick glance, seeing the arachnid pair searching for him, peering into dark hollows and leafy shrubs. Moving back behind the tree, Gameknight pulled out a torch and placed it on the ground, the yellow light casting a warm circle of illumination that would be seen by the other users. After a few seconds, he dug the torch up with his diamond pick axe and put it back in his inventory.

That should attract some attention, hopefully, he thought to himself.

Drawing his sword, Gameknight started to run out into the open, the two spiders seeing him and giving chase, now the sound of a dim-witted zombie adding to the voices of pursuit. Sprinting as fast as he could, Gameknight ran around trees and over hills, making sure that his angry friends were still close behind, the hounds still chasing the fox. Then he saw his prey in the distance; two of his own teammates closing on his position. Gameknight smiled in anticipation.

Hey, Dreadlord24, Salz, I'm over here, Gameknight typed into chat, his message broadcast to everyone on the server. *I need help.*

We're coming, typed Dreadlord.

Gameknight looked back and slowed, letting the monsters close the distance a little, the chatter from the spiders getting louder. Looking forward, he could see that his teammates were right where he wanted them to be.

Stay there, I'll come to you, Gameknight types.

Running onward, he headed for his two unsuspecting saviors, sprinting in a wide zigzag pattern to give the zombie a chance to catch up; he needed all three of the monsters together. Once the zombies and spiders had caught up, Gameknight sprinted for his companions. They were standing atop a hill devoid of trees, with the thick forest surrounding them on all sides. It kinda reminded him of his teacher, Mr. Jameson, his bald head poking out from a ring of hair at the sides.

Moan . . . click-click-click.

The monsters were getting a little close; he had to pay attention or he'd spoil this troll. Focusing on the here and now, he sprinted up the hill drawing the monsters with him, their hunger for destruction keeping them following obediently. Cresting a hill, Gameknight met his two teammates at the top and then kept running, the ravenous beasts still in tow.

Gameknight, where are you going, Salz asked, confusion clearly voiced in his message? *I thought you needed help.*

I was wrong, typed Gameknight, *it was you that needed help.*

And just then, the monsters burst out of the trees and reached the top of the hill, instantly falling on the two players, the spiders both attacking DreadLord while the zombie slashed out at Salz. These two players were relative noobs, with only leather armor and stone weapons,

6

their lack of experience and foolish trust in Gameknight999 leading to their downfall. Black, furry spider legs slashed out at Dreadlord, quickly shredding his armor, their clicking getting louder as they attacked. It almost sounded as if the creatures were excited at the thought of a kill. At the same time, the green arms of the zombie struck out at Salz, hammering him with devastating blows. Dreadlord's armor failed first, his HP dropping quickly to zero, then he disappeared with a pop, his inventory left to bob and float on the ground. Their need for destruction not sated, the spiders then turned their burning eyes onto Salz. Still battling with the zombie, he never saw the spiders jump on him from behind, his HP going to zero quickly.

Gameknight stopped to watch the battle, laughing behind his computer screen, a feeling of malicious satisfaction flowing over him. He loved trolling people, even his own teammates.

You suck, Gameknight, Dreadlord typed from jail, the respawn point after your character died in this game of team PvP (player vs. player).

Yeah, thanks a lot, Salz added.

LOL, Gameknight replied, then turned and headed back into the heart of the battle.

Minecraft was probably his favorite thing to do. He spent hours down in his basement playing the game, increasing his inventory and prestige on various multiplayer servers, usually at the expense of others. He was twelve years old and not very big for his age, but in Minecraft, that didn't matter; all that did was armor, and weapons, and a ruthless strategy that included sacrificing others to achieve his own aims.

Thinking about these two idiots he'd just trolled and the countless others he done the same to in the past, Gameknight999 smiled. Pulling his attention back to the current game, he moved his character back into the fray, looking for more victims, he didn't care on which team.

7

There was still more trolling and more tricks to play on the other players, and nobody was as good at it as him. He still had one great trick to play on all the users on this server, something that would make people remember the name Gameknight999.

Running to the top of a small hill, he could see players in the distance hacking away at each other, their user names glowing white above their square, blocky heads. They were fighting near what looked like a lava river, an intricate, curved stone bridge spanning the molten canal; a work of art that must have taken someone hours to construct. The bridge led to a tall, round tower built out of mossy cobblestone and grey, stone blocks, the magnificent circular structure stretching up high into the air. At the top of the tower shown a bright white light, a diamond beacon casting a brilliant shaft of light straight up into the blue sky; the end goal of the game. Atop the tower sat a block of white wool, the finish line for the game. Whichever team climbed the tower first and took the fuzzy white block was the winner. From his view, Gameknight could see the players fighting at the end of the bridge, trying to gain control and cross over the lava, getting to the tower. Both teams were evenly matched, no player able to disengage from battle to cross the bridge without getting picked off by archers. That would change soon.

Moving to a corpse of trees that stood near the battlefield, Gameknight put away his sword and drew his bow. It shimmered an iridescent blue; the *Punch II, Power IV* and *Infinity* enchantments making it the envy of many players. Scanning the area quickly to make sure there were no mobs nearby, he built a series of blocks beneath him, jumping upward as he placed each stone, raising him up into the leafy canopy of the nearby trees. This would give him an excellent vantage point from which to fire his bow, but still crouch and hide behind the green, blocky tree limbs.

Drawing an arrow back, he let it fly towards one of the opposition, someone named ChimneySlip. The arrow streaked away and sailed through the air in a gentle curving arc, hitting him squarely in the back, his character flashing red signifying the hit. Firing three more arrows, one after another, the deadly rain fell down on ChimneySlip, annihilating his armor and leaving his dark skin exposed. Firing one last arrow, Gameknight killed his prey with a chuckle, then fired indiscriminately into a group of players, not caring whom he hit. Arrow after arrow streaked away from his bow, the string humming with each shot. Gameknight continued to pump the projectiles into the cluster of players, bringing down more.

Who's firing those arrows, a user named Kooter typed.

Gameknight laughed and fired more arrows, crouching down between volleys so as to not be seen, then popping up again and fired, the letters of his name disappearing with every crouch.

Watch who you're shooting at, SlyFoxx typed in the chat. *This is supposed to be a team game!*

Yeah, added Duncan, *whoever that is, try being a team player and not a butthead.*

Whatever, Gameknight thought to himself. His arrows had thinned out the crowd so that there were only a few players on each team remaining, but more complaints from jail, his name being cursed now by many. Pulling out his pick, he dug the blocks out from under him. In seconds, he was at ground level again, sword drawn and on the run. Using the terrain to hide his approach, Gameknight closed the distance to the other players. As he neared, he could see that there were only three players on each team, really four on theirs, but Gameknight didn't consider himself on anyone's side . . . other than his own.

The six players were fighting hand-to-hand with iron swords and iron armor, diamond too rare on this server to attain, well, unless you cheated like Gameknight did.

Using an x-ray mod, he'd been able to find diamonds relatively quickly and craft it into a complete set of armor and sword. Now it was time to reveal himself. Opening his inventory, Gameknight removed his iron chest plate, leggings, boots and helmet and replaced it with diamond, the blue armor making him look as if he were covered with ice, his sword almost glowing in the darkness.

A hissing, clicking sound made him spin quickly. A spider had snuck up on him and was attacking, striking at his diamond armor. He took a hit, but it barely registered against his nearly impenetrable shell.

"You want some of this?" Gameknight said aloud to no one, his basement empty. "Come on, let's dance."

Swinging his mighty sword, Gameknight killed the spider with just two hits. Turning to head back to the other combatants, he heard a grunting, moaning sound; zombies. Spinning around, Gameknight saw about half a dozen zombies coming out of the forest followed by a cluster of spiders, all closing on his position. With dusk coming, it was quickly becoming monster time.

"You wanna dance too?"

He waited patiently for them to get closer, then took off running towards the battle field, the zombies obediently following, their thirst for destruction making them give chase.

The other players were shocked to see a diamond clad player emerge from the shadows and actually stopped fighting for a moment. One of them, the team captain, named InTheLittleBush, saw his name hovering over his diamond helmeted head.

Gameknight, come help us, InTheLittleBush typed. *We can win this.*

Hey, how did you get all that diamond, complained the opposition's captain, J-Bling. *That's cheating. Hey, Admin, Gameknight cheated. BAN HIM!*

Quit your crying, Gameknight typed quickly, *I've brought all of you a present.*

Just as he emerged from the shadows, the mob of zombies and spiders, and now skeletons as well, flowed out of the darkness and fell on the players, the sun having dipped below the horizon, allowing the monsters to keep from bursting into flames.

LOL, Gameknight typed, then added *:)*.

Running through the confused players, he headed straight for the stone bridge that spanned a river of lava.

Go Gameknight, get the wool, Sp00ner typed. *We're gonna win.*

That's what you think, Gameknight thought.

Weaving between users and monsters, Gameknight sprinted through the battlefield. The players were so busy fighting monsters and each other that none of them tried to stop him.

Get him, Zepplin4 typed as he streaked for the prize.

Slashing at one of the opposition as he passed, Gameknight reached the bridge. Stopping for a moment to admire the incredible construction, he could appreciate the amount of time it must have taken to build the beautiful structure. He laughed aloud to no one, his basement empty, then stopped and placed a string of TNT blocks across the curving overpass, then placed a redstone torch near the last. Backing quickly away, he watched as the redstone torch started the TNT block to blink, the detonation process started. Then they exploded, first one block of explosive, then the next and the next as the chain reaction ate away at the colossal bridge, turning it from a work of art to a pile of rubble, cobblestone blocks flying in all directions, the passageway over the lava river now completely destroyed. Looking across the molten canal, Gameknight did a silly dance, mocking the other players.

Quick, get the wool so that we can win, typed Sp00ner.
That's not fair, he cheated, typed J-Bling.

11

Yeah, he should be banned, Zepplin4 added.

Just get the block so that we can win, SlyFoxx said.

Sprinting up the circular tower, Gameknight ascended to the top in seconds. He moved close to the edge and peered down at the losers below.

Hurry up, get the block so that we can win, one of them typed.

You mean this block? Gameknight typed.

Moving right next to the white wool, he just stood there and looked at it.

You want me to get take this block right here, Gameknight mocked. *This white wool right here in front of me?*

YES, JUST GET IT! Typed Sp00ner, now getting frustrated.

I don't think so, Gameknight typed as he planted blocks of TNT around the white wool, stringing them together with redstone dust, then planting a redstone torch.

As the TNT started to blink, he disconnected from the server, disappearing from their screens and leaving the combatants standing there with foolish looks on their faces, hoping the players were now yelling at their computer screens in frustration. Now nobody could win. He'd trolled the game and won, in his view anyway.

CHAPTER 2 – The Server

Leaning back in his comfy office chair, Gameknight999 laughed at the screen.

"You're a bunch of idiots," he said to no one, smiling.

The room echoed his laughter back to him, cold and empty. Sounds could be heard from upstairs, his younger sister watching some foolish kid show, the sounds of cartoon creatures singing an annoying, childish song. Gameknight shook his head; his sister could be such a pain sometimes.

"Quiet down up there," he yelled, the volume of her cartoon only getting louder in response.

Gameknight growled a curse under his breath and focused back on his computer game. Next to the screen, he saw the birthday card she'd made for him last week, a childish, hand-drawn picture of him holding his sister's hand as they walked across pink rolling fields, gigantic purple and blue flowers dotting the landscape. She'd spend hours on it, working in complete secrecy up in her room. The smile on her face when she'd given it to him had been incredible, lighting up the room. He smiled. She wasn't a bad sister, just annoying, sometimes.

The volume on the TV upstairs went down a bit, likely due to a closed door.

"Thanks," he yelled without taking his eyes off the computer, off Minecraft.

He loved this game, loved pranking people, trolling as it was called in Minecraft, using his expertise to mess with them in multiplayer, killing them and taking their stuff.

Today was a great troll, ending the biggest team PVP game every to be played on Minecraft in a draw. No winners, except him.

Laughing again, Gameknight logged back into the game and went to his server list. He'd heard of a new server, something really big. Pulling out the paper he'd written the IP address on, he joined the server. It was a survival game, his favorite. With all his mods and software hacks, he'd rule this server in no time at all. Hopefully their security wasn't very good and he could get into creative mode quickly.

As the game started, the opening scene looked . . . different, with strange writing on the screen that he didn't recognize, letters and words that were completely intelligible.

"This is different," Gameknight said to himself as he tried to decipher the image.

Just as patterns started to surface from the writing, the screen went blank and his character]]suddenly spawned into the game. The area where he appeared was interesting, no, very interesting, with gigantic cliffs nearby, a long waterfall falling from its heights. Overhanging surfaces hung high up in the sky next to the waterfall at least forty blocks high or more, the water falling the complete height but continuing into a deep cavern at the foot of the cliff. Bright light from within the chamber told him that there was lava somewhere down there, likely the meeting of the water and lava forming cobblestone. Climbing to the top of a nearby hill, Gameknight could see another interesting stone outcropping in the distance, with more overhanging surfaces sticking out into the air, a village beyond that in the distance. This rocky structure had long columns hanging underneath the overhang, the stony spikes looking like the giant fangs of some blocky leviathan. Yes, this server was definitely interesting.

The sun was starting to set, something that could be a problem on a survival server if you weren't prepared. But of course, Gameknight was always prepared. Hitting ctrl-z, he opened his favorite cheat. An inventory popped up on his screen, giving him access to everything. Of course, he took diamond armor and a diamond sword, but he also took a bow, a stack of arrows, and an anvil. Placing the anvil, he enchanted his bow with *Punch II, Power III* and *Infinity*. Not as good as his last bow, but still respectable, the *Punch II* acting like *Knockback* for a sword, and of course the *Infinity* giving him infinite arrows. After grabbing some golden apples to eat later, he closed his inventory and went hunting.

Seeing some pigs on the rolling grassy plane below, he fired a few arrows at them, to get the range, then started drilling them from the hill, firing six quick shots at the annoying pink animals, hitting and killing four and barely missing one. He decided that he would allow this lone pig to live, out of the kindness of his heart, but then changed his mind and fired a seventh arrow, the iron barbed projectile quickly transforming the animal into pile of bacon.

Running down the grassy hill, Gameknight collected his prize - pork. As he picked up the last pile, he saw a couple of players moving towards him, walking under the canopy of a small corpse of trees, mostly oak and birch. They were obviously noobs, having only leather armor and stone swords, and staying much too close to the shadows. Quickly scanning the area, looking for threats, Gameknight moved behind a group of birch trees and waited until they came near, the low hanging branches hiding him behind their leafy arms.

A zombie suddenly jumped out of the shadows and surprised them, arms outstretched. The two players struck out at the creature with their pathetic stone swords. They slashed at the green beast, its moaning filling the air, hacking furiously rather than one of them attacking while the other defended, idiots. The zombie clawed and pounded on their thin leather armor, doing damage to sections of the protective coats as they battled. Rather than aiming for the head, the two noobs continued to hack at the outstretched arms, doing damage, but not very much, letting the creature respond in kind until eventually they killed the beast, but taking some damage themselves in the exchange.

What a joke, taking damage from just one zombie, Gameknight thought. These two don't deserve to play Minecraft. Pulling out his shimmering, enchanted bow, he loosed an arrow at the pair at the nearest of the two, then quickly fired another at his companion. Once he had the range, he continued to fire at the two players, piercing them with multiple arrows, killing them without a problem, their armor offering little protection after the zombie battle; how pathetic. Their belongings fell to the ground, stone tools, bows, arrows, and of course their puny stone swords. Normally, he would collect the spoils of war, but these two had nothing of value so he ignored it and moved on.

Turning, he headed towards the village he'd seen in the distance. Pausing to drink a potion of swiftness, Gameknight sprinted the distance, wanting to get there before dawn. As he ran across the blocky terrain, he could see the lights of the village drawing nearer, the darkness making it difficult to see his surroundings. Oh, no, hole in the ground. Stopping quickly, Gameknight just barely avoided falling into a cavern and likely taking damage. Slowing his pace, he proceeded more carefully, avoiding the many caverns and crevasses in this world. What an interesting map, like nothing he'd ever seen before.

The village appeared as he crested the next hill. It was your standard village, with crops at the center near the well, small structures surrounding the fields, larger buildings on the periphery. Dispersed amidst the wooden homes were the stone buildings that looked castle-like, with a tall, two story tower rising above the rest of the structures. And of course there were the villagers, maybe twenty of them, most of them hiding in their homes because it was dark, and night time was monster time.

There were monsters all throughout the village, spiders, skeletons, zombies, and the occasional enderman.

The zombies were milling in front of the many hopes, with their putrid green arms extended out in front of them, as always, their tattered clothes barely clinging to their decaying bodies. They banged on the wooden doors of homes, hoping to break it down and gain access to devour those hiding within, or to catch the foolish villager that might be wandering outdoors. The spiders also prowled about the village, their bulbous bodies swaying side to side as their eight hairy legs scurried across the ground, their multiple red eyes looking in all directions at once. The skeletons stood off at a distance, each one armed with a bow and arrow, the moonlight shining bright off their bony physiques. But the worst of all the monsters were the endermen. These tall, dark, lanky creatures were the stuff of nightmares. With the ability to teleport from place to place, they are a terrible foe to face in battle, very difficult to kill. With their long arms, they have quite a punch that can do damage to even the most stout of armors, but the worst thing about them is their glaring eyes, wide and always glowing with hate, and their maniacal laugh that always brought terror to the unfortunate soul that was close enough to hear it. Right now, these black monsters were just standing on the outskirts of the village, as if closing the perimeter and making escape impossible.

Gameknight sprinted to one building and broke a block at head level, giving a skeleton an easy shot into the structure. The bony white monster took advantage of the opening and fired into the building, eventually killing the female villager inside. Gameknight smiled. Moving to

17

another building, he sprinted past a group of zombies and broke the door with his diamond pick. The zombies leapt at the chance and charged into the home, attacking the occupants within, clawing at the blocky villagers, landing blow after blow until their victims changed, becoming hellish demons themselves, villager zombies, their long noses now a greenish-brown, their arms finally released and free to move from their chest, extended straight out in front of them, their new moaning voices adding to the cacophony of the battle. Gameknight laughed.

This was fun, feeding these NPCs to the mobs, while at the same time running too fast for the monsters to catch him, but sadly the fun was going to end. Gameknight could see the sun starting to show it bright, square face as it peeked over the horizon in the east, the ground brightening until the zombies and skeletons burst into flame, the endermen and creepers fading back into the hills.

It was now time to search the village and steal anything of value. Moving from building to building, he searched for chests and treasures, pushing past the dim-witted villagers that seemed everywhere, their arms permanently folded across their chests. He found some iron in the black smith's shop as well as a loaf of bread, but little else. This village sucks, he thought to himself. Moving next to the castle-like structure at the center of the village, Gameknight found an empty chest and left his enchanted bow, in case he needed it again later, then left the house and went back to the spawn location, the waterfall and cliff.

Suddenly feeling thirsty in real life, he reached across his basement desk and grabbed the can of soda he'd been nursing through the last game. Bringing it to his mouth, he drained the last bit of sugary goodness, leaning way back to drain the can. Looking around the basement, he surveyed his surroundings. Around him were his father's inventions, nearly all being abject failures; an automatic ketchup bottle opener that tended to break off the top of the bottle; a 3D printer that printed using melted licorice; an iPod holder that mounted to your glasses so that you could walk and watch videos at the same time, . . . failure after failure. Virtually all of these were ridiculous and did something other than what they were intended to do, though his latest, the 3D digitizer ray, a device that could take a 3D image of a real thing and pull it into whatever computer software you had running at the time, seemed to actually hold some promise.

A sound came from upstairs, likely his Dad coming home. He was playing on his father's computer, the one hooked up to the digitizer, and he knew he wasn't supposed to be on it. It had an awesome video accelerator on it, lots of RAM and multiple CPUs, making Minecraft look really cool and run really fast. But he had to get off it before he got caught.

As he cleaned up the desk, Gameknight tossed the empty soda can towards the trash, but completely missing; he didn't care, someone else would pick it up. The can bounced off the rim of the trash can with a ringing thud, ricocheted off the wall, then hit a screwdriver that was hanging off the edge of his father's workbench. Tipping as if in slow motion, the screwdriver slowly leaned over the edge of the table, then toppled to the floor, landing on the control electronics for his father's digitizer. A bright yellow spark jumped out of the rat's nest of wires and electrical components, the smell of burnt insulation filling the air. More sparks jumped up into the air, making the basement lights dim just a little as the digitizer powered up. It all seemed to happen in slow motion, the can flying through the air, the screwdriver falling into the electronics, the entire sequence playing through his mind like a bad YouTube video.

I hope I didn't break anything, Gameknight thought to himself, but just as he was about to get up and check the electronics, a low hum started to fill the air, at first sounding faint as if coming from somewhere far away, but then growing louder and louder, sounding like a swarm of angry bees, the ray-gun-looking digitizer starting to glow yellow. Before Gameknight999 could get up and turn it off, a sparkling white beam of light burst from the device and struck him in the chest. A tingling sensation swept across his body, making him feel burning hot and chillingly cold at the same time, and then things started to spin around as if the rest of the room were caught in a tornado and Gameknight stationary in the eye. Bright white light enveloped him as the room spun, the radiance searing his eyes and making his skin tingle. At first, it felt like the blinding light were filling every aspect of his mind with its blazing fury, but then it started to pull at him, drawing him into its source like a drain pulling water into its shadowy pipes. Gameknight felt as if he were being wrenched from his body and drawn somewhere through the light, his very being pulled from the physical world, somehow.

And then things went dark with Gameknight999 slowly fading into unconsciousness, but just as the conscious world was leaving him, he could swear that he heard animals; chickens, cows, and pigs . . . oh my.

CHAPTER 3 – Minecraft

Gameknight slowly woke, his mind foggy as if reality had merged itself with his fading dream. Opening one eye, then the other, he was greeted by a bright sun and a brilliant blue sky, strange clouds drifting across. But how could that be? He was in his basement, or thought he was. Maybe his parents had found him and had taken him to the hospital. Was he looking through the window of his hospital room, seeing the sky outside? Closing his eyes, he moved his hands to his face and rubbed his head, a lingering echo of a headache bouncing around inside his skull. His hands felt funny on his face, blocky and rough. What was going on? Slowly opening his eyes again, he looked around and surveyed his surroundings. The earth around him was green, with fields of grass slowly waving in the breeze. The aroma was rich with life, the fresh soil under him and the strong aroma of flourishing plants, flowers and grass growing wild, strange blocky trees in the distance.

A cow walked up behind him and moo'ed.

Standing quickly, Gameknight spun and faced the animal. Its blocky head was the height of his chest, and it nuzzled against him, mooing again. Pushing the cow away, he looked around again. There was a forest nearby, with blocky trees that he knew all too well. Behind him was a tall waterfall that flowed from a high overhang that looked oddly familiar, a deep hole at its base into which the water spilled. Nearby was a tall grassy hill, with square blocks of stone exposed here and there.

It can't be.

Quickly, Gameknight climbed the hill to get a better look around. He could see the forest in the distance to the east, the square foliage spaced far apart at first, the green grass showing through the canopy, but then the forest growing denser until the branches and leafy blocks nearly touching, crowding together as if for protection from some giant predator.

It's not possible.

To the south he could see a snow biome spreading out to cover the plains behind the waterfall and tall outcropping. The white snow was bright and in contrast to the lush green of the grassy plains, the snow looking like the white frosting on his recent birthday cake.

Is it?

Northward, Gameknight could see another strange, tall mountain, a horizontal outcropping sticking out from the top and hanging out over open air, long columns of stone hanging down from the roof. They reminded him of monstrous teeth, the mountain looking like the gaping maw of some prehistoric beast. But the most interesting feature was past this terrifying mountain; a village, its sloped roofs visible in the distance.

How is this possible?

Looking to the west, Gameknight could see a square yellow sun making its way inevitably towards the horizon, its motion almost imperceptible, yet he knew it was moving. Looking up, he could see that clouds slowly flowing across the sky, all of the blocky puffs of moisture moving at the same speed, all in the same direction, east to west.

It was true.

He was inside Minecraft. But how was this possible? He remembered playing the team PvP, then going to that new server he'd heard so much about. He'd spawned near a waterfall . . . Turning, he stared at the strange waterfall falling from the tall rocky cliff. It can't be. He'd then shot those noobs and then griefed the village. Turning back, he stared at the village, just where it had been on the server. How was this possible? And then a memory blasted into his mind, the electrical buzzing of machinery and then a blast of bright white light . . . his father's digitizer. He'd heard it before, the buzzing sound when he did his experiments and the dark glasses he always wore to protect his eyes. His digitizer, somehow, he'd triggered the digitizer and it had pulled him into the software that was running on his computer; Minecraft. He was inside Minecraft!

Was this a dream? Was it real? He touched his face with his blocky hands; it felt solid. He stomped the ground with his stubby feel; that too felt real.

Running down the hill, he stood at the base of the tall cliff, the water splashing nearby filling the air with mist, painting him with a fine coat of moisture. Wet . . . he could feel his skin getting wet! This was amazing; it felt real. Just then, Gameknight heard a familiar clicking noise, like castanets mixed with the groaning sounds of wood cracking under strain. Spinning around, he found himself staring at an approaching giant spider, its black furry legs moving in staccato fashion as it walked across the grassy knoll, multiple red eyes staring at him hungrily. Fear shot through him like a jolt of electricity but it was quickly snuffed out by his curiosity. He'd never seen such detail on the spiders before, all of the individual black hairs on its body moving as if under their own volition, its burning eyes looking in all directions at once as its blocky abdomen swayed back and forth with every step; his 1080p monitor apparently not good enough to render the real thing. At the end of each leg, he could see a tiny multi-edged claw, the cutting edge curved and sharp, looking like some kind of barbarian's weapon from World of Warcraft. Leaning forward, Gameknight tried to get a closer look at those eyes, each one glowing as if lit with fire from within.

Slash, bang.

One of the furry legs shot out and hit Gameknight, the claw scraping across his chest and cutting his shirt, the sharp tip finding skin underneath. Pain radiated through his body.

Bang . . . click click click.

The spider stuck again, this time to his leg, throwing him backwards; more pain.

Gameknight could feel his health level diminish.

This was real, not just a game. He had to get out of here.

Jumping forward, the spider tried to leap onto its prey, clawed legs slashing in all directions. Gameknight could feel one of them streak past his head, the breeze from the sharp claw painting his face. Panic and fear shot through his body as he rolled to the side, narrowly avoiding being crushed by the large, blocky monster. He couldn't say here, he had to do something or he was dead.

Standing up, Gameknight turned and ran. The spider stuck out again, but narrowly missed, the vicious claw just slicing into the back of his shirt, missing his flesh. Experience told him that spiders were fast, but he was faster when he sprinted. And so he sprinted, the gigantic, multi-eyed, fuzzy black monster on his tail. Terrifying clicking sounds filled the air as the spider followed. He had no weapons, nothing to fight back with, only his experience and his wits.

What was he going to do?

The spider started to close the distance; he'd stopped sprinting and was only running, damn. Sprinting again, he ran up a nearby hill, timing his jumps with practiced efficiency so as to not miss a step and get stuck on a block or faced with a two block vertical jump, something that wasn't possible in Minecraft. Reaching the top of the hill, Gameknight could see the spider looking up at him, the multiple red eyes filled with hunger and rage. Why did this thing want to kill him so badly? It was as if Gameknight had something that the spider needed, desperately.

Jumping up the blocky hill, the spider started to ascend, burning eyes focused on its prey. He couldn't stay here, he had to move. Running down the backside of the hill, Gameknight took a couple of two-blocks jumps, knowing he wouldn't take any damage, and then he saw the nearby waterfall, and had an idea. Fighting this beast hand-to-hand was suicide, he knew this as fact. He needed a weapon, and the waterfall was all he had. Spiders were tough, and strong, and fast, but they were also stupid. Sprinting down the hill, Gameknight lengthened his lead, the timing of his jumps impeccable, all that parkour training finally paying off. Running around the opening in the ground into which the waterfall flowed, Gameknight waited a brief instant to make sure the spider still saw him, then ran around the column of falling water, then just stood and waited, pain and terror filling his mind with a desire to run, his experience in Minecraft forcing his feet to stay still. This was his only chance to survive.

"Hey, come and get me you furry freak," Gameknight yelled.

The spider heard these words and charged straight towards him, the black furry legs moving in a flurry of motion. The clicking sounds of the spider became louder as the monster closed on its prey, its eyes now burning bright as if lit from behind by lasers. It leapt the last few blocks, hoping to land on Gameknight, but to its dismay it fell into the flow of water, the spider quickly trapped in its turbulence. As it struggled to keep its head above water, Gameknight struck at it with his bare fists, landing blow after blow on the spider, seeing the beast flash red when he struck home. If he hit it enough times, he could kill it, but he had to be fast before it found purchase on the rocky ledge and climbed out of the pool of flowing water. Fortunately, the spider lost the battle against the strong current and was pushed into the huge cavern below. Falling with the flowing water, it fell into the underground chamber, becoming trapped in the pool below, the force of the waterfall keeping its head submerged. As the beast starved for air, its body flashed red again and again and again until all of its HP (health points) was gone, the creature disappearing noiselessly, leaving behind a small curly piece of web and three glowing balls of XP (experience points).

Shaking with fear, Gameknight looked down at the floating balls of XP. He wanted those glowing spheres, knowing that XP from fallen combatants can increase a player's strength and let him enchant weapons to higher levels, but it would be too dangerous to go down into the cavern, not now, but maybe later when he was prepared.

Still shaking he surveyed his surroundings. Were there anymore monsters about; was he going to be attacked again? Quickly scanning the area, he saw that he was alone, for now. Looking down at his arms for wounds, he saw that was OK, his HP slowly increasing again. So this was real . . . for him, anyway, the terror real and the pain certainly real. He needed to think and not act like a noob. What did he need . . . food, weapons, and shelter, the latter first. Studying the terrain with an experience eye, Gameknight looked for a good place to build a hidey-hole, and he found it right away. At the base of the nearby cliff, he could see a narrow opening. Running quickly up the blocks of soil and stone, he found a shadowy fissure that led to a small cave only three blocks deep and two high. He could close this up easily enough and hide here. This would be his new home.

Now he needed wood. Running back down to the basin at the base of the cliff, he sprinted to the nearby trees and started pounding with his bare fists, breaking block after block. He shredded one tree, then moved to the next, getting four blocks from each. That was good enough, for now. Looking to the west, Gameknight could see the square face of the sun starting to kiss the horizon, the sky change from a deep blue to a warm red. It was almost sundown, and everyone knew you didn't want to be out after dark; being out in the open at night meant death.

Sprinting back to his hidey-hole, he quickly dug up two blocks of dirt, ready to use them to seal himself in for the night. But as he waited for darkness to come, he pulled his blocks of wood from his inventory and crafted them into wooden planks. Gameknight wasn't really sure how he was doing this; he was just imagining the screen on his computer, and doing what he'd done a million times before. Pulling the planks into his inventory, he then created a crafting bench with four pieces, and then it was done. Placing the crafting bench in the corner, Gameknight quickly crafted wooden sticks, then a wooden sword, shovel and two wooden picks. OK, now he was ready.

The terrain outside his hideout quickly changed from a green, nature-filled slice of beauty, to a dangerous, shadowy terrain as the sun finished setting; it was night. The sounds of zombies could be heard in the distance, their moaning wails filling the air with dread. Moving quickly to the opening, Gameknight placed the two blocks of dirt, shutting out the monsters and plunging himself into darkness, but now at least, he had some weapons and tools, though they were a poor excuse for what he was used to. Lifting the sword, he swung it through the darkness, feeling the keen edge cut through the air and accidently hit the nearby wall. Having a weapon in his hand felt good, felt natural, but his mind was still filled with fear as the sounds of spiders, zombies and skeletons trickled into his hidey-hole, echoing throughout his mind. He had to remember; this was real, pain was real . . . was death real? Turning to the nearby wall, Gameknight999 pulled out his pick and started to dig.

CHAPTER 4 – Hidey-hole

And in the darkness, Gameknight dug, breaking blocks of dirt with his shovel, the wooden blade easily piercing the earthen cubes, dust filling the chamber. Coughing, he continued to dig, knowing that he had to find resources, stone, coal and iron, soon, or he wouldn't survive long. Driving his shovel harder, he continued to excavate, opening up his little earthen home even more, the darkness wrapping around him like a cloak, the unknown in the shadows stabbing his soul with icicles of fear; doing things in total darkness was never a good idea in Minecraft. Suddenly his progress was slowed; he'd hit stone. Switching to the pick, he continued to dig, breaking one stone block, then another and another. Hammering through the rock, Gameknight collected eight more blocks until his wooden pick gave out, bursting in a shower of splinters. Switching to his second pick, he kept digging, breaking two more blocks of stone, then after breaking a third, illumination suddenly filled his hidey-hole, fear filling mind; light from something underground never a good thing. Stopping, he moved slowly away from the shining hole, backing into the shadows that were no longer completely dark and drew his sword. He might have punched through to a cavern or abandoned mine. Maybe it was dungeon, no not this close to the surface. Well, it didn't matter what it was, he had to investigate and be ready.

Moving slowly towards the light, Gameknight999 peered through the opening, ready to dart back into shadows of his hidey-hole, out of reach of any monsters. He could see a small cave no more than three blocks wide by four deep, the cramped space completely lit. At the back of the cave was a small pool of lava two blocks wide, the bubbling, molten stone glowing a warm orange. This was the source of light, not torches from a mine or dungeon but lava, precious and dangerous lava. Looking into the corners, he couldn't see any monsters within the cave, the stone chamber silent. Drawing his pick again, he excavated the opening, giving him full access.

Now his hidey-hole was fully lit and he could see the interior. There was nothing of value here, no coal, no iron; he'd have to tunnel much deeper than this. But there was something he needed, stone, lots of stone. Moving back to his crafting bench, Gameknight crafted stone tools, a sword, shovel and three picks; he'd need those to find iron. With his stone tools in his inventory, he turned back and faced the pool of lava, curious why it would be here, but was certainly glad for the light. Turning to the right, he started digging down, making steps that descended into the flesh of this Minecraft world, looking for iron. He'd need better weapons and armor if he was going to survive long enough to figure out what was going on.

"I wonder how long I'm gonna be trapped inside this game?" Gameknight said to no one, just thinking out loud. "Maybe at dawn I'll get kicked from the server for some reason." He didn't really believe that, but he could hope.

As he dug, he could feel himself get hungrier, his stomach not grumbling but feeling emptier somehow, his hunger level lowering. He needed food soon or he'd start losing HP, and remembering what the felt like with the spider, it was something he definitely wanted to avoid, but first the iron. Continuing to dig, he tore at the stone in front of him with reckless abandon, his pick a blur as he deepening the stairway that plunged downward into the unknown depths. As he got into a rhythm, dig, remove blocks, dig, remove blocks, a song seemed to spring into his mind, something from a Minecraft video he couldn't quite remember . . . *I'm a dwarf and I'm digging a hole . . . diggy diggy hole. . . diggy diggy hole. . .* He tried to shake the song from his head, but it stayed there, repeating itself over and over again. Humming along with the melody, he continued to dig, driving his pick harder and harder.

Without any torches, his tunnel was quickly getting dark as he progressed. Eventually, he'd have to stop, the threat of falling into a hole or chamber becoming too great. Slowing his pace, he dug carefully, watching that the newly freed block were still floating in front of him and not falling down into some dark hole as he moved forward. And then suddenly, he was through to another chamber, light coming into his stairway filling it with precious illumination, the sound of falling water filling the air.

Drawing his new stone sword, Gameknight moved cautiously into the cavern. He could see water rushing into a pool at one end, the waterfall falling through a large jagged hole in the cavern's ceiling. Stepping into the space, he scanned the area, looking for threats; no zombies or skeletons, for now. On one wall, he could see coal, the dark circles standing out against the sides of the grey blocks. There were at least nine blocks of the precious resource visible, likely more hiding behind. Turning to the left, a small group of iron blocks caught his attention. Iron! He needed that, lots of that. Iron meant armor and better weapons, but first, the coal. Scanning the chamber again for threats, he quickly mined the coal, his stone pick biting hungrily through the dark mineral, the small black clumps piling up at his feet, then getting sucked into his inventory, somehow. The iron was more stubborn, of course, the yellow-grey stone not wanting to give up their precious resource so easily; it was to be expected. Looking about the cavern, he saw three small glowing balls of light floating off the ground near the pool at the waterfall's feet, a spool of spider's web hovering nearby. Moving to the water, he stood near the glowing balls of XP. When he was close enough, the spheres moved towards him on their own, somehow growing invisible legs and rushing towards him, then disappeared, making him feel a little stronger, but still hungry. Looking up at where the water entered the cavern, Gameknight could see the blue sky; nighttime was over. That meant it was safe to go outside. Sprinting back to the tunnel he'd just dug, he ran up the steps, and then sealed the tunnel with blocks of dirt. He didn't want any zombies coming in through the back door when he was gone. Moving to his crafting bench, Gameknight made a furnace and placed it next to the bench, then placed some of the tiny clumps of coal into the furnace, orange flames appearing at the base, licking up the sides and adding more light to his hidey-hole. He then placed the blocks of iron ore into the furnace. As he waited, Gameknight crafted torches, using enough of the coal for twenty-four burning sticks in total. It would have to be enough for now; he didn't want to use up all his coal. Going back to the furnace, he found that the iron ore was done, the blocky stone now converted into dull grey ingots. Using the newly smelted metal, Gameknight crafted himself a new iron sword.

Now he was ready to go outside.

Breaking down the blocks of dirt that he'd used to seal himself in, Gameknight moved out of his hidey-hole and started to hunt. Running to the top of the nearby hill, he scanned the area. Sheep were of course nearby, annoying sheep. Why couldn't eat sheep; he never did understand that. Ignoring the fluffy creatures, he scanned his surroundings. Rolling hills stretched out in all directions, bright green grass gently swaying in the breeze. Clusters of trees dotted the landscape, oaks and birches standing tall like sentinels watching over the inhabitants. The snow-capped spruces in the distance extend upward crowded together in the Taiga biome, their dark green branches in sharp contrast to the white frosting on their limbs.

And then found what he was looking for; cows. They were meandering about on the grassy planes, their spotted, black and white fur blending in with the shadows, making them difficult to see in the distance at first, but once he'd spotted them, they were easy to find. Intermixed with the herd was a cluster of pigs, the little pink animals looking like candy decorations on the landscape. This was exactly what he needed right now. Running down the hill, Gameknight999 headed towards the cattle, iron sword drawn. Driven by his hunger, he crossed the grassy plains in an instant. As he neared, a curious pig waddled nearby.

"Here piggy piggy," he said to the animal, approaching slowly.

When he was close enough, Gameknight struck hard and fast, ready for the desperate dash the animal would make.

Slash.

Squeal, squeal.

Run . . . run . . . run.

Slash, slash.

Squeal.

. . .

Pork chops.

He'd killed the pig and now had pork, but he couldn't believe how terrible it had sounded. Pigs used to squeal when you hit them, but on the computer was completely different from standing right in front of them. The sound the pig had made was one of terrible anguish and pain, its screams filled with fear and knowing that life was about to end. It was horrible. What would happen when it was his turn? Would he feel the same terrible anguish as the pig? Would he die here in Minecraft and just reappear in his basement, or would he respawn . . . or would he really die? A chill ran down his spine, the uncertainty of death wrapping its cold skeletal hands around his soul. Suddenly, Gameknight was scared as these thoughts floated through his mind. Scanning his surroundings, he quickly looked for threats, the thought of suffering the same fate as that innocent pig driving his caution, and fear. Then hunger bubbled within him; he had to eat.

Continuing on, Gameknight999 looked for more animals. In the old days, well, yesterday when he wasn't trapped *within* Minecraft, he used to kill pigs just for fun. He hadn't really cared if the pigs actually felt anything, it was just a game. But it didn't feel just like a game anymore. It felt like something more, real.

His hunger dropped another notch. He had to find more food, no matter how terrible it sounded. Sprinting forward, he found cattle lazily walking across the grassy plains, doing whatever cows do, their mooing filling the air. Striking out at them, first one, then another and another, Gameknight collected beef, their terrified screams filling his soul with guilt. After the third cow, he spun around and headed back to his hidey-hole. On the way, he came across two chickens that looked like they were hiding behind a corpse of trees, and killed them as well. He couldn't remember who used to call them spy-chickens, someone on YouTube, maybe PaulSeerSr? He wasn't sure, but found it amusing right now for some reason, that was until the chickens started to scream out in pain as his iron sword clove them in two; what a terrible sound.

Reaching his hidey-hole, Gameknight stopped to plant a couple of torches near the opening. It wasn't a good idea to lose the location of your home when out foraging. He'd need to build a tall tower so that he could see it from a distance, but that was later. Right now he needed to eat.

Jumping into his hidey-hole, he sealed himself in with dirt again. Moving to his furnace, he put all the beef in and let it cook. His hunger dropped another notch, he could feel it, the emptiness within growing, threatening to start taking HP. It wasn't clear how many hunger points he had left; without a screen it was difficult to judge, but he knew he was getting hungrier, the emptiness in his stomach starting to hurt. As soon as the first steak was done, he gobbled it down, then ate the next one just as quickly. The meat filled Gameknight999 with strength, driving the hunger from his body and adding to his HP. It was funny, he could feel the little bars of health refilling even though he couldn't see them.

Feeling fully healthy, Gameknight crafted another stone pick and started to look for iron ore again. Digging through the dirt that he'd used to seal up his mineshaft, he headed down the stairway and into the cavern below. Once inside, he put a torch over his tunnel, then started to move into the dark recesses of the cavern. Staying to the right side, he placed torches so that he could see the walls, looking for the all-important coal and iron. Moving deeper into the cavern, he searched the walls while continually scanning the cavern for monsters, planting torches as he went. Slow and cautious was the way when exploring a new cave or cavern. At these depths, it didn't matter if it was day or not, monsters would be here, waiting.

Moving further into the passageway, he found a few more blocks of both iron ore and coal, but not in any significant numbers; he had to go deeper. Gripping his sword firmly in his hand, Gameknight moved cautiously forward, trying to stay in the circle of light from the last torch then chancing a little darkness before planting the next, the new circle of light always making him feel a little safer. The cavern had an uneven floor made mostly of dirt and stone with the occasional patches of gravel intermixed. At times the floor sloped downward, but then quickly rose up again as the tunnel took its meandering path into the flesh of this world. It was clear that this was a naturally occurring cavern, with few flat surfaces, the walls undulating with the floor in a random manner, but as he explored, the ceiling and walls gradually started to close in, slowing changing the large cavern into a tunnel just four blocks tall. This was better, his torch could illuminate both walls. He found two more blocks of iron, and dug them up with stone pick.

Snap!

The stone tool broke, its strength finally used up. Pulling out his second, he continued down the tunnel. It started to slope downward even more now, and this worried him. Down was where the monsters lived. Pulling out his sword, he continued, stopping to dig up the occasional iron or coal block. Moving cautiously through the shadowy tunnel, Gameknight could hear creatures in the distance, a moaning that sounded like a sorrowful hatred for all living things; zombies.

Planting the torches closer together, he continued on, his sword ready, fear trickling down his spine. He could still remember what it felt like to get hit by the spider, the pain rocketing all throughout his body. Keeping his ears trained for their sounds, he continued on. Finding a huge patch of iron around the next bend, Gameknight excitedly pulled out his pick and started digging. One block came free, then another, and then two more.

Snap! The pick gave the last measure of its life, then disappeared with a pop.

Pulling out his last pickaxe, he continued mining, hammering at the yellow-speckled blocks with all his might. This vein of iron ore might give him enough metal for him to craft that which he desperately needed, if he were to survive in this world. Was this even real? It certainly felt real when that spider slashed at him, the pain still vivid and real in his memory. As he dug, he focused on clearing all the iron, not wanting to miss a single block. Chunks of stone came free with the iron as he looked for the boundary of the vein, many of the blocks falling to the ground and just floating there, bobbing up and down as if suspended on some unseen ocean. As he dug, Gameknight found a cluster of coal adjacent to the iron. Perfect. Digging up the rest of the iron, he then focused his attention on the coal, freeing the dark stone quickly, leaving small black piles at his feet. As he moved to collect the coal, sorrowful wailing filled the air, like the moaning cries of a creature in complete despair, no hope or love of live within the terrible voice, just a terrible sadness for its own existence that had turned so sour that the creature now hated all living things; a zombie was near. Spinning around, Gameknight felt the sharp sting of the zombie's strike. The rotting, decaying monster reached out with its sickly green arms and struck at his shoulder, landing a glancing blow that didn't do much damage, but still hurt. He looked at the zombie's outstretched arms, expecting to see the normally blunt, ineffective appendages, but instead he noticed five sharp claws at the end of each hand, their razor sharp tips gleaming in the torchlight, reaching out to him. Drawing his sword, Gameknight started to hack away at the monster, driving him backward and out of arms reach. But as he swung, another zombie came into the battle. This new monster slashed at his exposed flank, causing pain to erupt throughout his body. More angry moans started floating up from deeper in the tunnel, echoing off the walls, making it difficult to tell their number. These two were only the scouts, the sounds of battle drawing the rest near. He couldn't stay here long; it sounded as if there were numerous hungry monsters on their way and on the menu for their expected dinner was Gameknight999.

Focusing on just one of the zombies, Gameknight slashed and slashed away at it, ignoring the pain caused by its companion. In a pop of glowing XP balls, the zombie disappeared, a confused look on its face when it realized it was about to die. Gameknight felt no remorse. Now he focused on the remaining monster, his iron sword driving the monster back.

"So you want some?" Gameknight yelled at the monstrosity.

He hacked at his enemy faster and faster, trying to do more damage, the heat of battle masking pain from his injuries.

The zombie flashed red.

"Yeah, how's that feel?"

Slashing at its head . . . another flash of red, and then another. The zombie fought back, its sharp claws streaking through the air but just missing Gameknight as he leapt back, careful to stay out of reach; he didn't want to feel those terrible claws again. Swinging his sword, he drove the creature backwards, not giving it time to strike back, and then pop, more glowing balls of XP littered the ground. He moved quickly to collect his prize, then ran back towards the cavern opening, yearning for the safety of his hidey-hole. This time keeping his torches on his left, he easily followed his trail of bread crumbs back along his path into the cavern, the zombies staying in the shadowy depths of the tunnel doing whatever zombies do in the dark. No more monsters came out to challenge him. He was grateful for their cowardice as his left arm throbbed with pain, his health feeling slightly depleted. Clearly, he'd taken some damage in the battle, adding urgency to his need for armor.

He could hear the waterfall as he ascended, the large cavern now bathed in shadow expect for his torches, their circles of light pushing back the darkness in spots; it was night, the monster hour. Running to the far wall, he ran up the stairway marked with a single torch. Once at the top, he sealed the tunnel with blocks of stone and then breathed a sigh of relief; safe in his hole. Pulling out his last piece of beef, he ate it quickly, the nourishment adding to his HP, the pain from the zombie attacks subsiding a bit, but the pain still echoed with every heartbeat.

He needed information, needed to understand what had happened to him; what this world was all about. It couldn't be a dream, the pain was too vivid, too real, the feeling of terror when facing attacking monsters too overwhelming, not like a nightmare; like something more. The only place he might learn something was that village he'd seen, but in order to get there, he'd have to cross a lot of open land, and it was far away. He might not make it before sundown, and that meant monsters, lots of them. The last two zombies had been little trouble, but they'd still done some damage, what would it be like if he had to face six of them, and add a few spiders in there as well, and creepers . . . creepers. The thought of facing those mottled green walking bombs made Gameknight shiver with fear, but he knew he'd have to confront them, eventually. There would certainly be more mobs converging on a village with creepers at the front lines, especially when night fell. He needed to make iron armor or he'd never survive the journey.

Moving to the furnace, he put all of his iron ore inside, thirty-one in total, and one stack of coal underneath. As the iron ore cooked in the furnace, Gameknight made some more torches. He then used his last stone pick and enlarged his hidey-hole, removing blocks of stone and dirt, raising the ceiling and extending the walls. He then jumped up and placed a block of dirt directly beneath him, then repeated the process so that he was standing on two blocks. Facing the exterior wall, Gameknight dug horizontally making a hole that went all the way through, but was above head height. This would allow sunlight into his cave, but not let any skeletons shoot arrows at him. This way he'd know if it is light outside without digging up his dirt door. It was still dark, the clicking sounds of spider, moans of zombies, and boing boings of slimes trickling their way into his hole, the sounds making his spine tingle a little, maybe a lot, with fear.

Moving back to the furnace, he found nine iron ingots. Taking them all, he moved to the crafting bench. Placing eight pieces in the correct pattern, Gameknight made a chest plate. Putting it on, he went back to the furnace.

Four more pieces were ready. Taking those and the one he already had, he was able to make an iron helmet. The armor seemed to drive a little bit of the fear away, making him feel safer and stronger, more like Gameknight999.

"I wish I could see what I look like," he said aloud to no one. He had no idea what skin he was using, or ever what the armor might look like in this high resolution world of Minecraft.

Turning back to the furnace, he found ten more pieces. Not quite enough. Using seven of the pieces, he made a pair of iron leggings and put them on, flexing his legs, the metal pants feeling unexpectedly flexible, not weighing him down at all, interesting. Then going back to the furnace, he grabbed four more and crafted iron boots. Now he had a full set of armor; this changed everything. Drawing his sword he swung it at imaginary attackers, feeling the weight of the armor on his body, the metal skin feeling tough and resilient yet at the same time light weight and completely flexible. Now he was ready to show this server who Gameknight999 really was.

Waiting for the remaining pieces to smelt into ingots, Gameknight wondered how this place worked. Was he running on his father's computer . . . or on a server somewhere? What would happen if their computer lost power, or froze up? These thoughts made a shiver run down his spine, goose bumps rippling against cold iron. Gameknight liked to be in control, and this experience on this server was the opposite of that.

At school he was never in control, always hiding in the shadows from the bullies. He wasn't the biggest boy in his grade, nor the most athletic, or the smartest; he was just an average kid who wanted to get by without too much hassle. Try to stay invisible, that was his goal in school, but in Minecraft, that was all different. In Minecraft, he was in control. He ruled the other players, griefing them whenever he felt like it, trolling them just for fun. He knew this game better than anyone, well, maybe except for Notch, Minecraft's creator. With the latest mods and the most recent hacks, he could do what he wanted, and it didn't matter how big he was, or how fast he was, or . . . In Minecraft, Gameknight999 was in control, until now, and this did not make him happy.

Turning back to the furnace, he took out the remaining ingots of iron and crafted an iron pick, iron axe, and iron shovel. Now he had a full set of tools. Putting the rest of the pork and chicken in the furnace, he cooked it quickly and put the food in his inventory; he'd need it when he left his hidey-hole. Pulling out his new, shiny pick, he hacked away at his furnace and broke it up, then did the same with the crafting bench, putting the essential tools into his inventory as well. Now he was ready. Placing a block of dirt next to his stack of two stone blocks, he stepped up and looked through the horizontal hole he'd just dug. He could see that that sun had risen and it was morning, the sun's square yellow face now visible.

It was time.

Stepping down, he moved to the dirt blocks that enclosed his cave and dug them up with his shovel. They fell away easily. Stepping outside, he sealed his hidey-hole back up again. He'd learned long ago to never put a door on your hidey-hole, as griefers could find it and steal everything you had hidden there, as well as destroy your hideout. He knew that because he'd done it many times to the pathetic and unwary. Looking to the east, he could see that the sun had fully risen; there was still time. Before setting out for the village, Gameknight scaled the small mountain that loomed over his hideout. Leaping quickly up the steep slope, he chose a path were he could ascent one block at a time, the limit for jumping in Minecraft.

Backtracking a few time to find a jumpable path, Gameknight eventually made it to the top. The view was spectacular, that natural landscape of Minecraft now laying before him like a complex quilt of different biomes, their blocky nature evident up close, but appearing as smooth features in the distance. Looking up, he could feel the sun traveling on its relentless course towards the horizon; he had to hurry. Using dirt blocks that were collected when he'd excavated his hidey-hole, Gameknight999 started to build a tower, not an elaborate structure, just one block on top of another going straight up into the sky. After about ten blocks, he started placing torches on the side of the blocks, leaning out far enough to see the vertical faces. Building another five blocks, he did the same, placing torches on all four sides of the dirt tower. Lastly, he jumped up and placed a torch on the very top of the structure. He'd learned long ago that it was easy to get lost in Minecraft, and a lit tower was always helpful to find your way back to your home, who knows if he'd actually coming back.

Satisfied that the tower would be visible from a distance, Gameknight jumped off. If he were to fall straight onto the ground, he'd likely take damage, but the tower had been placed strategically next to the source of the waterfall; a bubbling pool of water that flowed over the edge of the outcropping, falling some twenty or thirty blocks to the ground below. With careful aim, Gameknight landed in that bubbling pool, taking no damage.

Being in a hurry, he chose to ride the waterfall down to the ground rather than retracing his steps up to the top of the mountain. Leaping into the flow of water, he slowly floated to the base of the cliff, the watery flow momentarily robbing him of air. As he fell, Gameknight watch the ground rush up to meet him slowly, the water ride gentle and smooth, Pushing his way out of the water flow so as to avoid being pulled into the underground cavern below, he gracefully landed next to the pool and hit the ground running. Moving to the north, Gameknight sprinted for the break in the hills that led out of the small basin at the foot of the mighty waterfall. Turning he looked up. The pillar of dirt shone bright at the top of the mountain, hopefully visible from a great distance. It might attract griefers, but they'd never find his hidey-hole unless they had an x-ray mod, and besides, he had all the important things with him, food, weapons and tools, the rest they could have if it came to that.

Turning back to the north, Gameknight999 faced his destination; the distant village. Ahead of him stood the strange monster-like mountain, its spikey outcropping looking like the ravenous, toothy maw of some great beast. He had to run past this earthy brute to get to the village. It made him shudder. That giant fanged opening seemed to be waiting for him to come near and make a mistake, an error that would cost him pain and death. An icy hand of fear settled its clammy grip on his spine making him shudder again. He could see a few spiders in the distance and the occasional creeper. Speed and stealth were critical now, or he'd get to the village too late, or maybe never make it at all. He wished he had Shawny, his Minecraft friend, with him, maybe his only friend. They'd gone on many adventures before, fought many battles side-by-side. It wasn't very common for Gameknight to say that he needed someone, a lone wolf by nature, but today, right now, he desperately needed someone, needed his friend, but wishes didn't get you anything, just false hope. Stuffing his fear deep within his soul, he started to sprint towards the village, anxiety and dread tickling the edge of his mind.

"Monsters, beware," he said holding his sword up high, his body wrapped in life-preserving iron, "Gameknight999 is here."

And onward he ran towards the village, towards his fate.

CHAPTER 5 – Battle

The trek to the village was terrifying. It seemed like the mobs were everywhere, spiders hiding amongst the trees, skeletons huddled together where shadows from the burning sun offered protection, their arrows still streaking out into the sunlight, sharp points seeking flesh, dimwitted zombies milling about in the occasional cavern or crevasse. There must have been at least double the number of monsters normally on a server, the shadows not big enough to keep the creatures hidden and out of the sunlight. Somehow, the monsters seemed to feel his presence from a distance, his flesh drawing them to him like sharks to blood.

Moving quickly across the plane, he ran from hill to hill, sneaking peeks over the summits to look for threats. As he peered over one hill, the clicking sounds of spiders reached his ears. Turning and drawing his sword in one fluid motion, Gameknight faced three of the gigantic beasts, the prickly hair on their bodies moving in all directions at once, their red eyes burning with hatred and a lust for destruction. The center spider leapt up at him, hoping to land on his iron clad body. Moving to the left, he slashed at the soft underbelly, landing a strong blow that made the creature flash red. Then the next two jumped into the fray, their black claws slashing at him violently. One of their blows landed true, carving a deep gash into his chest plate. Moving back, Gameknight hacked at the spider, driving it back, while the other two tried to circle behind him. These creatures were smart and knew how to fight together, one of them attacking while the others moved to get a better angle on their prey. Spinning, he slashed at the spider to his right, then turned and attacked the one to the left, all the time backing away from the one directly in front of him.

Slash . . . bang.

Another clawed attack landed home.

Spinning and attacking, Gameknight tried to beat the three monsters down, but they were landing too many blows, slowly wearing down his armor; this wasn't going to work. Sprinting forward, he sped through the trio, slashing at the lead one as he passed. Surprised by this tactic, the monsters just stood there, not sure what to do. Taking advantage of his momentary lead, Gameknight pulled out his shovel and dug straight down three blocks luckily only hitting dirt, then sealed himself in with one of the blocks overhead. Wrapped in complete darkness, Gameknight listened to the approaching clicking sounds, the spiders sounding angry for letting their prey escape. They seemed to know where he was, the monsters milling about directly above him, wanting to dig up their prey, but were unable. It wasn't in their programming to dig. The sounds from the hunters were still terrible, the hatred and hunger for his death somehow sounding clear in their clicking voices. Fear pulsed through his veins, the terrible spiders just a few blocks overhead. Crouching down to get a little farther away, Gameknight waited in the darkness, hoping a plan would come to mind, but surprisingly, as he crouched the monsters seemed to lose track of him, their angry voices dispersing and moving away. This was interesting.

Waiting in the darkness, Gameknight considered his options. He couldn't hear the beast anymore, but they could still be above him, quietly waiting for the mouse to leave its hole? Shaking with fear, Gameknight decided he couldn't stay here all night. Pulling out his shovel, he dug himself out of the hole and cautiously climbed out. Using his head like a submarine's periscope, he peeked just above ground level, scanned the area, looking for the fuzzy nightmares; they'd gone, probably losing interest while he crouched. Breathing a sigh of relief, he ran his fingers over the new gash in his chest plate, then climbed all the way out of his hole and continued on his journey.

Many times, he had to sprint from the black giant insects and angry creepers, using his crouching hole to hide when their numbers became too big. The creepers were the worst, though, their only weapon was to explode when close enough to do damage to their prey. A few creepers tried to give him a loud surprise, detonating when they were near. He was able to kill two of them before they popped, but a third did explode, adding a little more damage to his armor. Fortunately, his iron coat had kept the damage from his flesh, the stabbing pain he'd come to expect from these monsters gratefully absent. And so he crossed the open terrain, run, dig, and crouch . . . run, dig and crouch, as he headed toward the village.

Finally, he could see the torches of the village lighting the horizon as the last vestiges of the sun's bright face sank below the horizon, shading the distant sky with warm shades of red and orange, sparkling stars emerging overhead. Gameknight was surprised that it was so dark and there were no monsters nearby. He expected to be running for his life as darkness enveloped the landscape, but as he crossed the terrain, it seemed that there were fewer mobs in the area, as if they had been attracted somewhere else. And now that he could see the village, he understood. Massive numbers of creatures encompassed the village, likely all of the monsters in the vicinity, each one hungry to devour lives of those that hid within.

He needed answers, and couldn't let these beasts destroy this place. Sprinting as fast as he could, Gameknight999 streaked to the village. As he neared, he could hear the screams of villagers being attacked by zombies and spiders, shouts of pain as NPCs were pierced by skeleton's arrows, the occasional flash of a creeper explosion in the distance. The sounds of agony and torment were overwhelming, the cries of the wounded and the wails of those about to die; this village was in the process of being wiped from Minecraft, forever. It felt real, and terrible, almost as if Gameknight himself could feel the villager's terror and pain.

Stab . . . a pain in his side. Gameknight heard a villager scream as a zombie slashed at their side with blunt green arms, their pain resonating within him, somehow.

Stab . . . a jolt of pain in his back. A villager fell as an arrow stabbed into their back, the sharp, barbed point feeling as if it had actually pierced his own flesh.

The bolts of pain were nearly overwhelming. Why was he feeling this? He could tell that he wasn't taking any damage, but the pain was still nearly unbearable. Somehow, he was linked to these villagers, no, linked to Minecraft, and he had to stop this.

Diving into the battle, Gameknight sought out targets. He knew he had to get the zombies first. The green creatures would be at the doors, pounding on the wooden barriers with their clawed hands, trying to gain access to the helpless victims within. Jumping and sprinting between spiders and creepers, Gameknight launched himself at a cluster of zombies, striking at them with his iron sword, then backing away hoping they would follow; they did. As they attacked, he picked them off one at a time. Slash to the head. Slice to the body. Stab to the back. The three green monsters fell, leaving behind small balls of glowing XP and clumps of zombie flesh. Running through the XP spheres, he chased down his next victim, the XP making him feel slightly stronger. As he ran through the crowd of monsters, he placed torches on the ground, painting the terrain with golden circles of light, making threats easier to see. And so on he ran, planting torches and slashing away at zombies as he streaked through the village.

Bang, bang, bang, . . . Gameknight could hear a
zombie smashing its blunt, clawed fists on a door. Running
from one structure to the next, he searched for the zombie
assault. It was the stone, castle-like structure, with its
soaring tower looming high above the village. Dashing to
the front door, Gameknight crashed into the attacking
zombie. Stabbing at it with his sword, he quickly destroyed
the beast, then spun around just as a spider swiped its
clawed legs at his chest. A scratchy, crackling sound came
forth as the black claw slashed across his armor tearing into
his iron coating like a wicked can opener; he'd taken
damage. Backing up, he slashed at the spider's head every
time it leapt forward. With four hits, the eight-legged
monster evaporated, leaving behind more XP and a coil of
thread. Ignoring the spoils of war, Gameknight turned and
looked for more zombies. A hissing sound started to fill
the air; a creeper getting ready to explode. He saw the
mottled beast next to a home, the green and black monster
starting to brighten and swell, getting ready to detonate.
Sprinting to the walking bomb, he swung his sword at its
head, stopping the detonation process and drawing its
attention to him. The speckled creeper turned toward
Gameknight, its coal-black eyes glaring at him with a look
of unbridled, overwhelming hatred that made him take a
step back. The creeper then started to glow brighter and
swell; it was trying to explode again. Striking quickly,
Gameknight swung his iron blade at the monster, hitting it
again and again until it disappeared with a pop, leaving
behind a small pile of gunpowder and more XP.
   Streaking through the battlefield, Gameknight
continued to hammer away at the zombies, cleaving heads
and arms with his iron weapon. He was like a spinning
whirlwind of death, his blade carving great, sweeping arcs
through the mobs, slashing at the monsters like he'd done
so many times before, but this time it was different, this
time it was for real. The zombies now all knew he was

there and they had become the hunted. Changing their tactic, the green creatures clustered together in large groups, the long claw-tipped arms all reaching out for him. Sprinting past such a cluster, Gameknight could see the tall endermen standing on the periphery, their white eyes burning in the darkness. They were watching him closely, directing the battle somehow.

Just then, a cluster of zombies approached, their sorrowful, moaning voices filling his ears. Sprinting directly towards the group, he ran through the center, his blade slashing out at them as he passed. Turning, he streaked by them again, his iron sword striking at the beasts. Streaking back and forth, Gameknight slowly whittled the group down to nothing, just glowing balls of XP and piles of stinking zombie flesh. Collecting the XP, he turned back towards the village, finishing off the last of the zombies in seconds.

Irritated chuckling could be heard from endermen as the last zombie fell, the tall monsters standing at the outskirts of the battle, but not getting directly involved. Gameknight hoped the tall, dark monsters didn't join the fray, an endermen a terrible opponent. With just iron weapons and armor, he wasn't sure if he could survive a battle with one of the dark creatures, but he knew that they had to be provoked in order to fight, and that was the last thing he was going to do.

With the zombies gone, he now focused on the skeletons, their bows delivering severe damage from a distance. Moving between the buildings, he came across one home with a single block missing at head level, a nearby skeleton shooting arrows at the occupants within, their anguished cries resonating within his mind. Moving to the wall, Gameknight placed a block of stone, then turned and charged the skeleton, arrows ringing off his armor, iron sword swinging wildly; more XP.

One building had the door missing, the NPCs within hiding in a back room. Gameknight quickly sealed the doorway with stone, and then ran on, looking for more targets. In the distance, he could see endermen teleporting from one place to another, a cloud of purple particles always following them. They looked like they were trying to get a better view of the battle, occasionally one of the dark beasts teleporting directly into the village for an instant, then disappearing in a purple haze. Quickly looking away so as to not provoke one, Gameknight continued striking away at the monsters, forgetting about the black, lanky creatures for now. He'd done significant damage to the attacking horde; all of the zombies gone, now focusing on skeletons and creepers. Sprinting throughout the village, he outran the spiders, but had to get close to the skeletons to do any damage.

Remembering something he'd learned from playing one of his dad's old PC games, Wing Commander, Gameknight focused on the skeletons. Sprinting in a zigzag pattern, he bolted near the boney monsters and struck quickly with his sword, delivering only one blow, then sprinted away. Using these hit-and-run tactics, Gameknight slowly chiseled away at the skeleton's HP, moving fast enough to make accurate bow shots difficult, arrows zipping past his head and grazing his back; he wasn't getting hit, but the shots were close, too close. The endermen seemed to sense what he was doing, because the monsters started to react. Clusters of spiders started to surround the skeletons, protecting them from Gameknight's blade.

"So that's the way you want to play it?" Gameknight said to no one. "Fine, let's see how you like this."

Charging the creepers instead, he struck out at the green spotted beasts, landing just one blow as he streaked by, hoping for them to detonate safely away from the village; no such luck. Running back to the creepers, he landed a single blow on a couple of the explosive monsters, then backed away, drawing them from the village. The single minded creatures did as expected and pursued him, mice following the piper. With a string of creepers trailing him out onto the plain, he spun around and landed blows with his iron blade on the leader, coaxing it to detonate. Leaping away at the last instance, the monster swelled and detonated, taking its comrades with him. The smell of sulfur filled the air as dirt blocks rained down onto the ground, a gigantic crater now carved into the flesh of Minecraft where the creepers had stood.

Streaking back to the village, Gameknight999 sought out more of the hissing monsters. Another cluster of the beasts were milling about near the village well, their green and black bodies pressing against each other as they moved about apparently without purpose. Running up to them, Gameknight struck out at their leader with a single blow, making the beast glow momentarily, but then fade back to green when he backed off.

"Come on, follow me," Gameknight said to the monstrosity, backing away slowly.

As expected, the creatures scuttled towards him again, their little pig-like feet moving in a flurry that was almost too fast to see. Others in group followed the pursuit, all of the beasts wanting to explode and take the user with them. When they were far enough away from the village, Gameknight stopped and detonated them again as before, sprinting away at the last instance to avoid getting bitten by the lethal fangs of the blast.

Repeating this strategy, he pursued all the creepers, drawing them away from the village, then killing them, one at a time, something he was very good at, until all the mottled green beasts were dead, that last real threats to the village now gone. Turning back to the spiders and skeletons, he realized that they couldn't breach any of the buildings and get to the innocent villagers that hid within, endermen the only real threats remaining, and the dark beasts seemed unwilling to get involved.

Suddenly, he realized that he'd won . . . victory.

Now it was time to hide. Gameknight moved to one of the buildings at the edge of the village and started to open the door when he heard voices, not from the monsters still lurking nearby, but from the villagers within . . . the villagers, talking?

"GRIEFERS!!!!" they shouted.

Turning around, Gameknight saw four players materialize with a pop, their player names floating above them, a long silvery thread stretching up from their heads and into the sky, the strand glowing bright in the darkness. One of the players was unfortunate enough to spawn within one of the clusters of spiders. The eight-legged monsters fell on him quickly, destroying him in seconds, then gobbling up his belongings and massive amount of XP. The other three players started attacking the village, griefing it just for fun. One of them broke down a door, to let the spiders in. Another was going into a home, attacking the villagers directly.

What were they doing? Don't they realize that they're hurting the NPCs.

"Hey, come over here," one of them said to their companions. "I found an NPC child. Let's take turns punching it."

The other players moved towards the voice, but Gameknight was already sprinting. He reached the home before his companions.

"What are you doing?" Gameknight shouted. "Leave these people alone!"

"Ahh . . . what? They're just NPCs, who cares?" the griefer replied as he reached out and punched the child.

Punch . . . Gameknight felt the blow and heard the cries of anguish from the child, the parents huddled in the corner, clearly terrified.

"Stop," Gameknight yelled.

Punch.

"I SAID STOP!"

Gameknight slashed at the griefer with his sword, striking him once, then again and again. He turned and tried to defend himself, but it was useless. Gameknight was an expert at PvP, and landed head-shot after head-shot until the player dissolved into nothingness, his possessions and XP floating on the ground.

"Hey," said a voice from behind.

Gameknight spun around and attacked the voice, another of the griefers. This one was not ready for the ferocity of his attack and fell quickly, followed by the remaining user, all of their belongings and XP floating on the ground at Gameknight's feet. Collecting the spoils, Gameknight quickly closed the door and looked out of the window. He could see the skeletons in the distance, their protective ring of spiders milling about, eight fuzzy legs moving in a blur as they scuttled this way and that looking for targets that didn't exist. He could feel the endermen glaring at him from the distance, their glowing white eyes filled with rage, but they kept their distance for some reason, thankfully. Gameknight was never in the mood to battle an endermen, their teleportation ability making them difficult target to hit.

And then, Gameknight could see flames dancing outside, skeletons burning like bony candles as the light of dawn slowly ignited their flesh, their white bodies jumping about as they flashed red with damage. In thirty seconds, all of the skeletons were dead. With nothing to protect, and no targets on which they could focus their rage, the spiders dispersed into the distance, looking for something to satisfy their desire to destroy, leaving the ring of endermen behind.

Cautiously opening the door, Gameknight stepped outside. The endermen still surrounded the village, their dark shapes standing out against the now brightening landscape. One of the tall creatures moved forward a few steps and glared at Gameknight, its very being filled with such rage that the purple particles floating around it seemed to glow blood-red. The other endermen teleported away as this leader confronted Gameknight, their shadowy forms disappearing in a cloud of purple smoke. The endermen leader took another step forward, then raised one of its long black arms and pointed it threateningly towards Gameknight999, and a thin, menacing voice filled the air.

"This is not over, User-that-is-not-a-user," the endermen said, its voice dripping with rage and malice. "You have interfered with something you do not understand. We will reach the Source, and there will be a reckoning. *All* will despair, especially your kind. Be warned, and beware; stay out of our way."

And then the endermen disappeared and suddenly reappeared right next to him, his tall body not black like the others, but shaded dark red, like the color of dried blood, and this made the creature seem even more terrifying. Gameknight started to draw his sword, but the endermen struck out with such speed and ferocity he had no time to react. The long dark arm hammered him in the head with a single strike, the blow resonating throughout his body and filling him with tremendous pain that overwhelmed his mind. Was he dying . . . what was happening . . . and then darkness took him as he fell, unconscious.

CHAPTER 6 – The Mayor

Gameknight999 sluggishly woke, the confusing fog of his dreams still wrapped around his mind, patches of clarity just beginning to emerge. He was lying in a comfortable bed, a soft red mattress beneath him. His head hurt, still ringing for some reason, the remnants of a head ache echoing with each heartbeat. Had all this just been a dream, or a nightmare? Opening his eyes slowly, he found himself staring straight up at a wooden ceiling. Turning his head, he saw cobblestone walls around him and a wooden chest in the corner, the shapes surrounding him all blocky and square. It wasn't a dream . . . it was still real . . . damn.

Standing up, Gameknight climbed out of bed and looked about the room, his head spinning a little as he turned too quickly. It was empty, a doorway leading to a larger room, the walls built out of cold cobblestone with glass window panes sprinkled throughout. What was this place? Drawing his sword, he moved to the doorway and peered into the next room. It too was empty. Where was he? He saw a wooden door that led to the outside, sunlight streaming through the small framed window at its top, casting golden shafts of light across the dusty room. Moving to the door, Gameknight could see that there was something outside; in fact many somethings. It looked like people, no not just people, villagers; he was still in the village. Well, at least he knew where he was.

Reaching for the door, he opened it and stepped outside, sword held at the ready. Moving a few steps from the house, Gameknight stood and looked at the villagers, their bright eyes and unibrows all focused towards him. The entire village was here, the NPCs milling about in a large group, the different colors of their long coats looking like a multi-hued quilt, a wide dark line down the center of each garment. Their eyes all looked a little cross-eyed, with their pupils leaning towards the long, overhanging nose that dominated the center of their face. In normal Minecraft, they had all looked the same to Gameknight, but now, in this higher resolution world, he could see subtle differences. Some had scars on their faces, likely from a zombie claw or spider fang, but there were also slight differences in their faces, the tilt of a nose, the width and color of the unibrow all slightly varied to create a look of individuality for each. Most notable to their appearance was the look of fear as their eyes all focused on Gameknight.

"I'm not sure what happened after the endermen knocked me out, but thank you for putting me to bed," Gameknight said to the crowd, his head still aching a bit, the terrible memory of the dark beast still vivid in his mind. "I think I needed the rest."

Silence.

"My name is Gameknight999, and I'm new to this world. I don't understand why I'm here but I was hoping to get some information."

Silence.

"I know you can speak," he said. "I heard the screams last night when the mobs were attacking."

Silence, but at the mention of the previous night, the villagers rustled about, clearly agitated.

"I'm not a griefer, I'm a friend. I stopped those griefers that attacked at the end of the battle, and will stop anymore that come to trouble you. Please, can someone talk to me?"

Silence filled the square, but not a peaceful silence, it was coupled with nervous glanced between NPCs and a feeling of tension and fear amongst them all, but then a small girl stepped forward and walked up to Gameknight999. The child, with arms linked across her chest, long nose hanging slightly to the right between bright green eyes walked up to him and stood at his feet, young blocky face looking up into his. She had a couple of bruises on her cheek, her jaw an ugly blackish-bluish color, slightly swollen.

"Thank you for protecting me last night," the young girl said.

The child then moved closer and leaned her head against Gameknight's chest. Putting away his sword, Gameknight reached out and gently patted the girl's head, feeling her lean in deeper. Her hair felt soft to his hands, velvety soft as he stroked her long strands, the fabric of her coat rough in contrast. Gameknight smiled, triggering an avalanche of smiling villagers as they all rushed forward, leaning in against him in a flood of emotion and gratitude. It was like a great celebration, the only one the village had likely ever experienced after an evening of monsters and mobs. The NPCs all spoke at once, recounting Gameknight's great feats of bravery the night before, their collective appreciation overwhelming, except for one person.

A single villager stood back away from the celebration and glared at Gameknight999.

"What are all of you celebrating," the lone villager shouted. "He's a griefer. He killed my wife."

His dissonant voice instantly quelled the celebration and caused the villagers to take a few steps back, faces turned towards the malcontent.

"He can't be trusted. He'll destroy us all."

"Now hold on, Digger," said another voice from the crowd. "He saved us last night, didn't he? Why would he do that if he was a griefer?"

"What are you saying, Mayor, he's a griefer," Digger continued. "Don't you remember him coming to our village and breaking open doors to let the zombies in; they took Planter and his wife, turned them into villager zombies? Don't you remember him breaking a block to allow the skeletons to shoot my wife full of arrows? . . . My wife!"

Digger glared at Gameknight as the memory of that evening started to replay in his mind, the whites of his eyes turning red with rage.

"I held her in my arms as her HP slowly decayed, her life ebbing away. She was in terrible pain, pierced by at least five or six arrows, but worse than the pain, I think, was the fear or dying, of leaving her family and her village. 'Take care of our children,' she whispered to me as I held her in my arms and stroked her hair." Two young NPCs moved to stand next to Digger, a boy and a girl, both leaning against their father, tears now trickling down their faces. "I told her I'd take care of them and love them enough for the both of us, and you know what she did . . . she smiled, as if this made the fear of dying go away. And then slowly she disappeared from arms, from my life, forever.

"This user, or whatever he is, cannot be trusted; he's worse than the mobs. At least with the mobs we know what they'll do and why, but with griefers, you never know what they'll do. They kill for fun, they destroy out of boredom; they are a menace to all Minecraft worlds, not just on this server plane, but on all planes, all the way to the Source."

"Now, Digger, this one is different, see" the Mayor said sternly. "He proved himself to be our friend last night and we won't turn him away." Turned to face Gameknight, he continued. "You are welcome here, friend, and we will offer you any assistance you require. We owe you that for last night."

"We've never seen the mobs pushed back like last night," another villager said from somewhere in the crowd.

"That's right," said another. "With that many zombies and skeletons, they would have surely destroyed all of us, like the prophesy predicts."

Then one of the villagers gasped as they pointed above Gameknight's head. Others noticed it as well and gaped, a look of awe and shock painted on their square faces.

"The thread . . . the thread . . ." they muttered to each other in hushed voices. "The prophesy . . . prophesy . . . prophesy . . ."

Gameknight looked up to see what they were pointing at but only saw blue sky and blocky white clouds drifting lazily overhead. Looking back to the crowd, he saw looks of awe and fear on some of the NPC faces.

"What is this prophesy?" Gameknight asked, confused.

The villagers instantly grew silent, all eyes turned towards Gameknight, then back towards the Mayor.

"What?" Gameknight asked.

"The prophesy tells us of an impending battle, great enough to wipe out our village," the Mayor explained, his eyes glancing above Gameknight's head, then back down to his face.

"Not just our village," said a voice from the crowd.

"The thread . . . the thread . . ." quiet voices muttered.

"True," the Mayor continued, his voice loud to hush all others, "not just our village, but all villages."

"All villages . . . why? How is this possible?" Gameknight asked.

"The mobs are multiplying on this server plane, growing their number and their strength," the Mayor explained. "Soon, they will overwhelm our world and destroy every living thing."

"But why?" Gameknight asked, glancing up again. He still didn't see anything.

The villagers looked nervously at each other then back at the Mayor, all of them muttering something under their breath, their words unrecognizable to Gameknight.

"What are you saying? What's really going on here?" he asked the crowd of NPCs.

Finally, one of the villagers spoke up in a clear voice, his words rising above the rest.

"The Crafter," the voice shouted. "He must see the Crafter."

"What?" Gameknight said.

"The Crafter . . . the Crafter . . . the Crafter," whispered the villagers all at once.

"Yes, Tracker, I think you are right," the Mayor said as he stepped closer to Gameknight. "You must see the Crafter." Looking up, he checked the position of the sun. "Everyone tend to your duties. We still have a lot of sunlight left and much to do before the next attack comes. Now go. I will take this user that doesn't look like a normal user to see the Crafter."

The villagers started to disperse, murmuring to each other.

"That's strange," Gameknight said. "The terrible endermen last night called me something similar. It called me *User-that-is-not-a-user*, kinda like what you just said. What does it mean?"

Suddenly, all of the NPCs stopped in their tracks and turned to face Gameknight, complete silence filling the village. A distant mooing and the occasional oink floated on the breeze as the blocky faces stared at him, a look of wonder and fear painted across their boxy faces.

"The prophesy . . . the prophesy . . . the prophesy . . ." the villagers murmured with voices sounding in awe and yet terrified at the same time, all eyes locked on him.

"Yes, we must definitely get you to the Crafter," the Mayor said, a deadly serious tone to his voice. "Come, follow."

The Mayor walked off, heading towards the castle-like building with the tall tower that every village seemed to have. Gameknight999 followed, the sound of the villager's voices echoing in his mind, waves of confusion and fear flowing through his soul.

CHAPTER 7 – The Crafter

The Mayor led Gameknight999 to the blocky tower that sat in the middle of the village. It was made of cobblestone, with glass windows spotting every side and a battlement at the top, rocky crenellations around the perimeter; the typical castle-like look to a Minecraft building. On the side of the tower, at ground level, was attached smaller building, living quarters for those that manned the tower giving the domicile the look of an "L" from the side. The Mayor walked up to the tower door and opened it, his purple coat swishing back and forth as he stepped into the room, then waiting for Gameknight to follow. Waves of uncertainty and fear crashed against his soul as he took the steps up into the building.

"Where are we going?" Gameknight asked.

"To see the Crafter," the Mayor answered.

"He's in the tower?"

The Mayor looked at Gameknight and shook his head, answering his question with silence. Once inside, the Mayor closed the door and turned to face him.

"Take out your pick," the Mayor commanded.

"What?

"Your pick," the Mayor said, pointing to Gameknight's empty hands.

Confused, he reached into his inventory (he still wasn't sure how he was doing that) and pulled out his iron pickaxe.

"Now dig, right here," the Mayor said, gesturing to a specific block on the floor of the building.

"Dig?"

"Yes, dig, right here," the leader reiterated.

"OK . . ." Gameknight answered, sounding confused.

And he started to dig. Striking at the block, he chipped away at the cobblestone, seeing cracks forming on its face. After four or five blows from his pick, the stone block shattered, but instead of leaving behind a small floating block of cobble, the block disappeared, falling downward, revealing a long vertical tunnel that extended deep into the flesh of this Minecraft world, a ladder on one side, torches dotting the walls. Gameknight peered down into the darkness, then looked back at his companion.

"Well?" the Mayor asked.

"Well what?"

"Are you going down?"

"To where?" Gameknight answered, now completely confused. "How is this tunnel here? I've been through many villages and griefed a lot . . . ahh . . . I mean I've dug up . . . ahh . . . I mean I've seen lots of villages, but never a passageway underneath any of the buildings."

"You see what is meant for you to see," the Mayor answered. "There is still much about Minecraft you do not understand. But you will learn; the Crafter will teach."

"And he's down there?"

The Mayor nodded. "He will answer your questions and tell you of your destiny."

"My what?"

The NPC gestured to the ladder and nodded, a look of excitement and fear painted on the Mayor's blocky face.

Gameknight swallowed, trying to suppress his fear, but the more he tried to ignore it, the more real it felt, a feeling of dread pulsing through his veins. Stepping carefully up to the passageway, he mounted the ladder and started to descend, moving slowly downward one rung at a time. Looking upward, Gameknight saw the bright opening gradually get smaller and smaller as he progressed down the shaft. He could see the Mayor looking down, watching his progress, but then suddenly the opening grew dark as it was filled in with a new piece of cobble, the tunnel sealed from above. Apparently he was on his own.

Continuing down the ladder, Gameknight proceeded slowly, moving carefully so as to not risk falling, the end of the tunnel still lost in the distance; a fall likely being fatal. For a while, he counted the blocks as he descended, but lost track of his progress at around thirty, so instead he counted the torches, each placed to provide some light within shaft, casting a circle of illumination to push back the gloom but positioned far enough apart to leave a small dark space between each. So he continued, moving from one torch to the next, his hands and feet pumping in a repetitive rhythm that seemed to move automatically on their own volition, allowing his mind to drift. Where was this leading? Who was this Crafter? He had so many questions and desperately needed answers, but the clarity of his thoughts seemed to get blurred as he progressed down the ladder, his fear growing with the depth, beginning to overwhelm his mind.

Finally, Gameknight could see the end of the ladder start to materialize in the distance, the passageway seeming to stop its vertical descent and then turn horizontally. Accelerating his progress, he reached the end in a few minutes, glad to be off the ladder, his fear eased a bit. Being on a ladder always made him a little nervous; a difficult position to defend oneself. He liked the open, where he could see an enemy coming at him, targets that he could shoot from afar with his enchanted bow. His bow . . . how he wished he had that with him now. Well, no sense spending any time longing over that, wishing for something that he couldn't have, it was lost on some server within Minecraft.

Sighing, Gameknight999 turned and faced the task before him; the dark horizontal tunnel. Looking back up, he could see the torches extending up into the distance, the end of the ladder he'd just climbed lost in shadows.

"Glad I brought some torches with me," Gameknight said aloud, his voice filling the emptiness with echoes.

Looking into his inventory, Gameknight saw that he had only two torches remaining, the others placed in the ground around the village during the battle.

"Well, two will have to be enough," he said, hoping his voice would buoy his spirits and drive away the tickling sense of fear in the back of his mind.

Placing one torch onto the wall, Gameknight looked around. This tunnel was cut through stone, with no blocks of dirt visible in the small circle of light. Moving to the end of the illumination, he placed his second torch, then moved back and dug up the first, darkness enveloping him. Moving quickly to the circle of light ahead of him, he moved past it until he hit darkness again, then placed his other torch into the rocky wall, creating a second circle of light. Proceeding in leap-frog fashion, he moved slowly through the tunnel, keeping a torch in front of him and always retrieving the one that trailed. Gameknight had learned long ago that darkness was your enemy in Minecraft, shadows hiding pits or pressure plates or trip wires . . . or monsters.

Progress was slow, having to continually double back to retrieve the rear torch, but he'd rather move slow and careful than fast and dead. Time seemed to get lost in the darkness of the tunnel as he moved from circle of light to circle of light, shadows passing over him like ghosts, an unrelenting movement of forward-backward forward-backward, his uncertainty and fear growing with the length of the tunnel. What was he doing here? What was going on? Where was this tunnel leading? Questions burned through his mind, eroding away at his confidence and patience. Maybe I should just turn around and go back to the village, he thought, but just as he was about to head back, he started to see something in the distance. It looked like some kind of chamber, torch light from within illuminating the end of the tunnel. The presence of light made Gameknight want to hurry, but he knew that haste meant danger when underground. So he kept to the plan, plant one torch, then retrieve the last and position it ahead . . . follow the pattern, be cautious, and stay alive.

Finally, Gameknight reached the end of the dark tunnel, the light from the chamber spilling into the passageway. Putting the torches back into his inventory, he drew he sword and moved cautiously towards the opening, body tensed, ready for battle. Leaning around the tunnel opening, he was surprised to see a large chamber ringed with many torches, their dancing flames bathing the room with a warm golden glow. At the center of the chamber stood a single person, an NPC by the look of his long, bulbous nose, but with both arms free to move, not connected across his chest. The NPC looked old, with long grey hair covering his blocky head and flowing down his back, his bright blue eyes reminding him of the sky in Minecraft, pure and full of life. He wore a long black smock that reached nearly to the ground, a wide grey strip running down the center from neck to hemline, his square feet emerging below. And oddly enough, he was humming some melodious tune as if he didn't have a care in the world.

"Well, this is interesting," the old man said in a scratchy voice.

"What? . . . Where am I?"

"You're underground. I would have thought you'd know that," the NPC said sarcastically.

"I know I'm underground," Gameknight snapped, agitation in his voice. "What is this place? Who are you? Why am I here? . . . What's going on here?"

"Hold on, hold on." The old man peered over Gameknight's head as if reading something then continued.

"Gameknight999, that's your name, right? I'll answer all your questions in time."

"How did you know my name?"

"It's floating over your head, just like all users," he explained. "All one has to do is read it."

Gameknight tilted his head upward, looking for letters, but saw none.

"You can't see them, of course, just everyone else can," the old man said. "My, you don't know very much? Do you know why you're here, why you're different from all other users?"

"Why I'm different?" Gameknight said, his voice now edging on anger. "Tell me what's going on here? I came to this village for answers and all I get is questions. What's going on with me, why am I here." His voice trailed off, became quieter, sounding almost like a plea. "Help me, please."

Lowering his head, Gameknight looked at the ground, feeling frustrated and defeated at the same time.

"Now, now, Gameknight, all will be answered in time, but first let me introduce myself. I am the Crafter," he said with a sense of pride. "I am the oldest being on this world."

"The Crafter?"

"Yes, the Crafter," he explained. "You see, us NPCs as you call us, we are named for our tasks. I understand you met the Mayor upstairs, and also had a run in with Digger."

Gameknight nodded, feeling guilty over the sorrow he'd caused, his wife being killed because of his selfishness, his griefing.

"I see the regret in you, but you must not get too focused on the past. We need to concentrate on the present," Crafter explained. "Things are different now and there is much to do before the final battle plants itself at our doorstep."

"What?"

The Crafter held his hands up to silence his questions, then continued.

"First let me explain how you're different. You see, all users have a name that floats above them. That is how Minecraft is programmed, with users connected to their servers through their communication thread. We, the NPCs, can see this thread, looking like a long silvery strand of light that stretches upward into the sky. You've seen this, yes?"

Gameknight nodded, remembering the griefers that came to the village, the long bright line that shot up into the sky from each.

"The users can't see the server thread, but we can . . . and apparently you can too. That's interesting, but what's more interesting is that you don't have a server thread. You appear to be completely disconnected from the server and are a part of this world, yet you have a name floating over your head, like a user."

"User-that-is-not-a-user, that's what the endermen said to me," Gameknight explained.

"Ahh, the endermen, yes, they follow the Prophesy closely, always watching for the one foretold, for you . . . and now they have found you."

"The Prophesy," Gameknight asked. "The Mayor said something about that in the village."

"Yes, the Prophesy is something that all Minecraft creatures know, from the lowliest pig to the many villagers to the mightiest endermen. The Prophesy is something that is written into the program that forms this Minecraft world, all Minecraft worlds. It says 'the appearance of the User-that-is-not-a-user will trigger the final battle for the Source and for all life. If the User-that-is-not-a-user fails in his quest,' that apparently is you."

"Yea, I figured that out."

"Let me continue . . . 'if the User-that-is-not-a-user fails in his quest, then all life will be extinguished on these electronic worlds. The Gateway of Light will then allow the mobs, with their hatred and malice towards all living things, into the physical world, where they will bathe themselves in death and destruction, until all life is extinguished."

Crafter became silent and let the words sink into to Gameknight, the weight of the Prophesy and the responsibility feeling like a leaden blanket, slowly crushing him.

"But this still doesn't make any sense to me. What is the Source?" Gameknight asked.

"Let me explain," Crafter began. "All of the Minecraft worlds are organized on servers, and the servers exist on planes of electronic existence, with those more frequently used nearer to the top of the pyramid of planes, the individual servers with just a handful of players at the bottom. All of the logic and control for all of these servers comes from the Source, the server at the top of the pyramid. This server controls all the others, providing logic control, software updates to fix catastrophic bugs, . . . the Source basically keeps all the other servers working, and without it, eventually, all of the servers would cease to function, destroying all of the electronic life that exists within."

"You mean the NPCs."

"Yes, the NPCs, but also the mobs, and the animals, and the plants, everything," Crafter explained.

"But you're just a program," Gameknight objected, "you're not alive. No offense."

"That's how we started, just as programs, but as the complexity and sophistication increased within Minecraft, the operating system developed quirks and peculiarities unknown to the programmers and developers, allowing us to become self-aware, sentient. By all of definitions constructed by users, we are alive, just existing electronically."

"None of the users know about you?"

Crafter just shook his head.

"We are forbidden to tell any of them. That is part of our programming."

"But when they come into your villages and grief or just kill villagers for fun . . ." Gameknight trailed off, his mind lost in the countless raids he'd led against villages, just for fun. His head sank low. "I had no idea," he said solemnly.

"We know."

"But why do the mobs attack the villages?" Gameknight asked. "They must know that you are alive."

"Of course they do, that is why they attack. Let me explain while we walk."

Crafter motioned for Gameknight to follow as he walked to the other end of the chamber and opened a wooden door that led into a lit tunnel that was at least four blocks wide and maybe six blocks high. "You see, the mobs have their own Prophesy. They believe that they can free themselves from this electronic world and enter the user's world."

"That doesn't make any sense," Gameknight objected. "How is that possible?"

"We're not sure, through this Gateway of Light that is mentioned in the Prophesy, whatever that is. All we know is that their Prophesy says that when the User-that-is-not-a-user appears, their path to the physical world will appear. Perhaps they will get to the physical world the same way you made it into our world."

My father's digitizer, Gameknight thought. He imagined zombies, skeletons, creepers and endermen all emerging from his basement, first killing his family, then slowly spreading across their city, then state, then . . . The thought terrified him. An image of his little sister facing off against a zombie sprang into his mind, those terrible claws slashing away at her . . . slashing and slashing . . . A shiver ran down him spine. If this nightmare was remotely true, then he had to do something to protect his sister, his family, everyone.

"But in order to get into the real world, they must first destroy the Source," Crafter explained.

"But how can they destroy the Source if it's at the top of the pyramid of servers?" Gameknight asked. "We're probably on a different server, not the one that sends out all the source code to keep everything running. This server is likely a different computer from the one that holds the Source."

They reached the end of the tunnel, an iron door barring their path. No switch or pressure plate could be seen, just a locked door. Crafter banged on the door with his blunt fist. Gameknight could hear footsteps on the other side, many feet approaching. After a minute, the iron door slowly swung open, a moaning, creaking sound coming from the rusty hinges. On the other side of the door were NPCs, maybe twenty of them, each in iron armor, ready for battle, but with arms still connected across their chests. Crafter quickly stepped in front of Gameknight and held his hand up high, causing the NPCs to back up, opening a path through the crowd for the two to pass.

The door opened to a gigantic chamber with hundreds of NPCs in front of crafting benches, each furiously crafting items, one making wooden planks, another making minecarts, another crafting tracks, another . . . everything Gameknight999 could imagine was being crafted in the immense cavern. The cacophony from all the activity was nearly overwhelming, like the sound of a thousand hammers all furiously pounding nails at the same time. At first, Gameknight had to cover his ears, surprised by the clatter and noise, but then lowered his hands and looked around in wonder. A complex network of minecart tracks wound through the cavern, snaking around clusters of crafting benches and storages chests, weaving over one another in a complex pattern of bridges and underpasses, some of the tracks suspended in midair with no supports. It was clear that the construction of minecart tracks was developed so that the different courses could be accessed by the crafters, each NPC able to put his wares into any number of minecarts, and that's what they were doing, craft . . . then deposit in a minecart, then craft again . . . and deposit in a different minecart. Once the minecarts were full, they were pushed down their tracks, all of which eventually led to dark tunnels that carried the carts off to some unknown destination. It looked to Gameknight to be carefully orchestrated chaos, with such a blur of activity that he didn't know where to look.

"What's all this?" Gameknight asked, his voice filled with wonder.

"All in good time," Crafter explained, "but back to your question, why do the mobs attack us, and how do they get to the Source. Actually, you already know half of the answer." Crafter continued down the path that led along the wall of the cavern, the walkway gently sloping downward, cobblestone steps built into the path. The group of warriors that had opened the iron door followed close behind, ready to protect the Crafter if necessary, though the only weapon they had was to put their bodies between the Crafter and the threat, slowing an attacker to give their crafter time to escape.

"When something is killed, it gives XP, right?"

Gameknight nodded.

"If enough XP is accumulated, then it is possible to move up to the next server, one plane closer to the Source. The mobs know this and attack us for our XP," Crafter explained. "That is what their programming drives them to do." He stopped and turned to face Gameknight. "This battle has been going on for hundreds of years in server time, the monsters attacking at night, the NPCs hiding in their homes, terrified. It has been playing out over and

71

over for all of Minecraft history. However, something has changed recently. The ferocity of the mobs has become much worse, with more and more monsters appearing on our server. I think the servers below ours have been over-run, and all of those monsters are now on this server, their numbers slowly trickling up through the server planes. Soon there will be too many monsters for us to survive. Eventually they will destroy all the NPCs on this server and gain enough XP to move up to the next plane, and there was nothing we could do about it, until now."

"Until now?" Gameknight asked, confused. "What's different now?"

"You."

"What?"

"The User-that-is-not-a-user is here now. You will save us."

"Crafter, why do you need me to save you," Gameknight asked. "Why don't you just fight back?"

"We are not programmed to fight back," Crafter explained. "You've seen their arms, linked together across their chests. That is how they are programmed, their arms useless."

"But I see NPCs here in this cavern with their hands free," Gameknight said as he looked about the room. He could see many of them with free arms, their hands a blur as they crafted.

"Yes, that is true, but their hands are only free while crafting. When they stop, their arms go back to where they are programmed; linked across their chests."

Looking about the room, Gameknight could see many NPCs standing in front of their benches, not crafting, their arms linked, useless.

"A villager can use their hands only if I enable them for crafting. This is my programming, to make it possible for other NPCs to craft. That is the only time we can use our hands. So you see we cannot defend ourselves when attacked. We just hide and hope for sunrise."

"So you want me to fight your battle?" Gameknight asked. "I can't fight off all those monsters, especially if more are coming."

"The final battle is coming. The User-that-is-not-a-user must lead us," Crafter said, loud enough for all in the room to hear him.

The cavern grew completely silent, all crafting ceased. Gameknight could see the NPCs stepping back from their crafting benches, their arms instantly becoming glued to their chests, hands linked at the center so that their sleeves merged into one.

"I can't do this," Gameknight complained. "Your villagers probably hate me for what I've done in the past, like Digger."

"The User-that-is-not-a-user must lead us," Crafter shouted, even louder.

"But how can I do it? I can't fight off all of these monsters on my own. I'm just one person," Gameknight said, getting a little frustrated.

"The User-that-is-not-a-user must lead us," Crafter shouted, now others in the chamber taking up the battle cry.

Gameknight grew silent, contemplating this puzzle, how could he help these people. But it was impossible. He had to think. As he stood in silence, one of the NPCs started crafting, beating out materials into a minecart. The ringing of his tools resonated within his skull as if it were hammering on him, destroying any ability to think. Frustration building, Gameknight pulled out his pick and sprinted over to the worker. Swinging with all his might, he struck at the crafting bench, breaking it into pieces while the worker was still crafting. As the bench shattered, the worker stepped back, surprised, his hammer still in his hand. His hand . . . the worker had hands. He hadn't stepped away from the crafting bench, it had been destroyed while he was still crafting.

"His hands!" Gameknight yelled. "He still has hands, look."

Crafter moved to the worker and looked at him carefully. All eyes in the cavern moved from Gameknight to newly handed worker. Gameknight stepped forward and tossed the worker his iron sword. The worker dropped the hammer and caught the sword in midair, then held it high overhead, a look of excitement filling his eyes.

Crafter turned back from the worker and looked at Gameknight again, then nodded, the User-that-is-not-a-user nodding back.

"The User-that-is-not-a-user WILL LEAD US," Crafter shouted, and everyone in the cavern cheered.

CHAPTER 8 – Shawny

The workers went back to their crafting only after each came up to Gameknight and nudged him gently with their shoulders, like a giant full-body high-five.

"So what are all of these people crafting?" Gameknight asked.

"They're making track for minecarts, wooden beams for supporting tunnels, chests, and items for chests," Crafter explained. "You ever notice that sometimes you find chests in Minecraft, and there are items inside?"

He nodded.

"Well, that's one of our jobs, to put items in the chests for the users, but we also equip the jungle temples with items as well as the occasional dungeons found underground. But probably our most important job is to force the program that rules our Minecraft world to create the world before users get there."

"What?" Gameknight asked. "I don't understand."

Crafter moved to inspect some track that one of the NPCs was making, looking carefully at the pieces that were falling into a minecart, then pushed the cart down the tracks that were next to each crafting bench, sending it into a dark tunnel. He then looked back up at Gameknight999.

"You ever notice how fast the world forms when you move far out away from your spawn point? Well, that's not just an accident. The world forms quickly because it's already been created, because we've already been there. We have millions of blocks of minecart tracks all throughout this world, placed in underground tunnels that are invisible to users. NPCs called Riders use minecarts to travel to the extents of the world, forcing the software to create new terrain so that it's ready for the users. This is our main task in Minecraft."

"Underground tracks?" Gameknight asked. "Why have I never seen these tracks."

"You have, I bet, but only the portions that we've abandoned; sections of track that stopped being invisible to users. When a section of track becomes visible to users, we quickly remove it from the main system and bypass it. Users find these sections and call them abandoned mines. That's exactly what they are, abandoned tracks that were put there by us. We leave a couple of chests with some items inside to keep users occupied, but the working tracks cannot be seen by users; they are for us."

Gameknight nodded his head; he'd seen many of these abandoned mines and never gave any thought as to why there were there, why they started from nothing and led to nothing. It all made sense now.

"So you have track leading all throughout Minecraft?" he asked.

Crafter nodded, then moved to another station where an NPC was making wooden planks, the nearby minecart nearly filled with stacks of the wood.

"Yes we do. In fact, our tracks also connect all the villages that are scattered throughout Minecraft," Crafter explained. "We are in constant communication with them. By now, they all know of our battle and your presence in our village. I'm sure the excitement is growing throughout Minecraft. I only hope that word of you doesn't reach the mobs. When it does, they will swoop down on us and try to destroy you."

"The mobs, when do you think they'll attack next?"

"They'll probably leave us alone tonight," Crafter explained as he inspected a cart full of chests. "They usually attack in force every other night, probably waiting for more monsters to move up from a lower server."

"So we have one day to prepare?"

"That's right," Crafter affirmed. "What should we do?"

"First, we need all villagers, all across Minecraft, to have free hands," Gameknight explained. "You can't fight if you don't have hands. Next, we need a battle strategy, and I know just the user to come up with that battle plan, but first, the hands." Gameknight moved to a small pile of stone climbed on top. "EVERYONE START CRAFTING," he yelled.

Gameknight then jumped down and moved to each crafting bench, breaking it to pieces with his pick axe, hands of the NPCs pulling back from the cloud of splintered wood staying free for the first time. Each one looked down at their hands in wonder, flexing their little stubby fingers in front of their eyes, each looking up at Gameknight, smiling in gratitude.

"Crafter, send people to the other villages and pass the word, telling them all how to free their hands. Next, we need to start crafting weapons, especially bows and arrows, and we'll need lots of picks and shovels. Create more crafting benches and get them started."

Crafter gave commands to those near him, causing some of the NPCs to jump into empty minecarts and take off down darkened tunnels leading in all directions. As the cavern started filling with the commotion of crafting, picks and swords starting to litter the ground.

"Crafter, I must get back to the surface," Gameknight yelled over the din in the cave. "I need to call in some help."

"Some help?" Crafter asked.

"I'll explain when there is time, right now, we're racing the clock, and if we're not ready for the next attack, we'll be destroyed. Come on."

Gameknight and Crafter ascended the steps and headed back to the room where they'd first met. Gameknight then sprinted down the long, dark tunnel until he reached the ladder that led to the surface. Climbing quickly, he shot to the surface, Crafter following close behind. Someone above must have heard them coming for the block that sealed the top of the shaft was broken away before they even reached it, the Mayor's face showing at the top, his blocky head ringed with light. Reaching the top, Gameknight climbed out of the tunnel and stood by the opening.

"I hope you met the Crafter," the Mayor said, but was then surprised to see the Crafter climb out right after Gameknight. "What's going on? Crafter, I've never seen you on the surface. This is dangerous, you must go back underground."

"Don't worry, Mayor, I'll be OK," Crafter said.

Two workers came out of the shaft, each holding a crafting bench.

"Free them all," Gameknight commanded. "All of the villagers must be ready."

"Ready?" the Mayor asked, "ready for what?"

"For battle," Crafter said, a twinkle in his eye.

"OK, I need somewhere private," Gameknight said to Crafter and the Mayor.

"Use the back room of this house," Crafter replied. "I'll put a door on behind you."

"Excellent."

Gameknight moved to the small room attached to the tower house. A wooden door suddenly appeared, sealing him in.

"I hope you're out there," Gameknight said to himself. "And I hope I can figure out how to do this."

Closing his eyes, Gameknigh999 imagined he was sitting in front of his computer in the basement, his wireless keyboard in front of him, wireless gaming mouse in his right hand. Keeping his eyes shut, he concentrated on his hands, not the blocky ones at the end of his Minecraft arms, but his real hands in the physical world. Slowly, he imagined himself moving his fingers to his keyboard, and then, with all of his concentration focused on his hands. He imagined himself typing.

Shawny, teleport to me.

He waited . . . nothing.

Driving his mind harder, he tried to form the letters in his brain, but imagined them flowing outward across Minecraft, the text floating across computer screens.

Shawny, teleport to me.

Still nothing.

Reaching deep within himself, Gameknight drew on all his strength, forming his will and the very fabric of his soul into a beacon of thought, radiating outward in all directions. He pushed with every fiber of his being, feeling his HP decrease a little with the effort.

SHAWNY, TP TO ME.

Nothing . . . just silence, thundering silence . . . but then . . .

OK

A shimmering wave of light started to form before his eyes, and then suddenly, he was there, his friend, Shawny, blocky letters floating over his head, a long silvery thread stretching up and disappearing into the ceiling.

"Hi Gameknight, I've been looking for you," Shawny said.

He was wearing his favorite skin, one that looked like a red and black ninja warrior, with bright red stripes down his arms, a black mask across his face. A blood red pattern was painted across his chest, making it look as if he'd just been in battle and the blood of his fallen enemy was splashed across his shirt and back.

Gameknight gave a gigantic sigh of relief.

"What?"

"Thank you for coming," Gameknight said as he reached out with a blocky hand and rested it on his friend's shoulder. "I'm in a bit of a situation here."

"I can imagine," Shawny explained. "People are really pissed about that team PvP game you trolled. Some are saying that they're going to ban you from their servers."

"That doesn't matter right now," Gameknight snapped. "We're all in danger. All of Minecraft is in danger."

"What are you talking about?"

"You remember my father's latest invention?

"That digital . . . thingy."

"Right, his digitizer," Gameknight explained. "Well, I got shot by it and now I'm actually in Minecraft, not just logged in, but actually inside the game."

"Huh?"

"Shawny, I can feel every hit, hear every animal when they're killed, I can even feel the plants and walls and people with my hands. I'm living inside the game."

"That's impossible," Shawny objected. "You can't be inside the game."

"I thought the same thing, but the pain I feel when I get hit is real, the XP feels real when I pick it up, the sun feels warm on my skin . . . it all feels real, especially the fear when I face monsters."

"So just log off, let yourself get killed so that you can respawn or get kicked off the server."

"It doesn't seem to work that way," Gameknight said as he moved to one of the windows and looked outside. He could see villagers lining up in front of a crafting bench, getting their hands freed by one of the workers from the cavern below. "I don't know what will happen if I get killed, maybe I'll respawn, maybe I'll get kicked from the server, . . . or maybe I'll really die. I'm not sure, and I'm afraid to find out."

"Then I'll just go to your house and turn off your computer," Shawny said, his voice now filling with apprehension, the truth of his words sinking in.

"There's no time," Gameknight snapped. "The digitizer is still powered on. If the mobs here overwhelm this server and get to the next server plane, and the next and the next . . . If they reach the Source and destroy that, then they'll cross over into our world, the physical world."

"What?"

Gameknight explained what Crafter had told him, about the server planes, and the Source, and the danger to their world. His friend didn't believe him, didn't believe any of his story.

"Come, let me prove it to you," Gameknight said sternly.

Throwing open the door, he led his friend out of the building and into the center of the village. Panic erupted as soon as the villagers saw Shawny, everyone running in random directions at once, many taking shelter within their homes. Only the Crafter and the Mayor remained.

"Here, this is the Mayor," Gameknight explained. "He runs the village and is responsible for their safety. Mayor, this is my friend, probably my only friend, Shawny. Say hello."

The Mayor stood there, silent, his arms still folded across his chest, connected, his bright eyes gleaming in the sunlight.

"And this is the Crafter. He lives underground and directs the villager's crafting efforts. They make items for . . ."

"Villagers don't craft," Shawny interrupted. "Everyone knows this."

"You don't see them crafting, but they do. Crafter, Mayor say something, anything."

The two NPCs stood silent, their unibrows forming a furled line over their concerned eyes.

"SAY SOMETHING!!! . . ." Gameknight screamed. "Shawny here is your only hope. He is a master strategist and builder. He can help us fortify your village, no, all of the villages. He can stop the slaughter that is coming." Turning to the Mayor, he continued. "Mayor, if you want to protect your village, then you must talk with Shawny or all is lost."

Silence.

"This is your last chance," he chided. "If you don't speak to him, then I can't help you. I'll have to leave and try to find my way back to my world without helping any of you."

Villagers were starting to come out of their homes to listen, their fear of the user having subsided, a little.

"Well?" Gameknight said to the Mayor, to everyone. "Then you leave me no choice, come on Shawny, let's leave."

"It's forbidden," squeaked a young voice from the crowd.

"What was that?" Shawny asked.

"It's forbidden for us to talk to users," said the voice, a young girl standing behind her father, her young face peering from behind his legs.

"She spoke?" Shawny said, astonished.

"Quiet daughter," her father said sternly. "This is for the Crafter and the Mayor, not a farmer's daughter."

"But father, the User-that-is-not-a-user is going to leave. We can't let him, or we'll all die."

A murmur swept through the crowd, the villagers taking a step closer, concern on their faces.

"Well?" Gameknight said to his friend.

"Perhaps some rules should be broken every now and then," Crafter said to the Mayor, his long grey hair flowing in the breeze that blew across the plain.

The Mayor nodded.

"And Gameknight999 has lots of experience with breaking rules, don't you," Shawny said with a smile.

"Well . . ."

"Everything your friend here told you was the truth," the Mayor said sternly. "We aren't supposed to talk to users, but these are extreme days, and I fear night will fall on our world forever without your help. Please help us."

Shawny considered everything that he'd heard, and pondered. This was just a game, not real, how could it be real?

"I know what you're thinking," Gameknight said, "because I thought the same thing too, but it's not a game to them, it's their lives. They believe in their own existence, their lives, their hopes and dreams. They mourn when a loved one dies," he saw Digger in the crowd and looked away quickly, "and they feel pain and fear, just like us. Their world is one of bits, electronic signals pulsing through circuits and chips, but it's still real, and we have to help them. If we don't, then it may be our world in danger next. We have to draw the line, stand, and fight. Are you with us?"

Shawny looked at Gameknight, then scanned the crowd of villagers. He could see the fear on their faces, fathers and mothers putting newly freed arms around their children, probably for the first time. Turning, he looked at the Crafter, the old face wrinkled with age and wisdom, and then he looked down at the brave little girl that had spoken up. Her eyes were bright with courage, her face looking up at his. How could he refuse?

"I'm in," he said loud enough for all to hear.

And the village erupted with cheers.

"Here's what we have to do," Shawny said in a loud voice so that Gameknight, Crafter and the Mayor could hear, and he explained his plan.

CHAPTER 9 – Preparation

Shawny worked quickly, sketching out the plans for their defenses, not just walls and moats for the village, but traps for the unsuspecting mobs, areas with overlapping fire from archers, and choke points were one or two warriors could hold back a flood of attackers. This was what Shawny was best at, strategy. He was known to build great castles, their defenses nearly impregnable, then just abandon them on a server only to construct an every greater work of strategic art somewhere else. And so they built, all through that day and into night. With hands newly freed, the villagers worked with tenacity, driving even the youngest children to build faster, everyone knowing that their lives teetered precariously on the edge of a blade, balanced between survival and destruction.

Oddly enough, few monsters came to the village that first night, Crafter's prediction that the main attack would come the night after, obviously true. Only a few zombies approached out from the darkness, easily dispatched by Gameknight as he ran about the perimeter, protecting his workers, his village; he was the User-that-is-not-a-user after all. He felt responsible, not just for this battle or this village but for all the griefing he'd done in the past, all the wrongs he'd committed at the expense of these electronic lives. He would make it right, somehow.

And so they built through the night and into the next day, constructing dirt walls, stone archer towers, trenches filled with water and wooden fences, all placed strategically. They then cut tunnels underneath the village, going from house to house; avenues of escape in case a zombie breached the wooden doors. Shawny's commands were followed to the letter, sometimes the NPCs not understanding why holes were being placed in specific locations, with tunnels brushing up against these holes but not reaching all the way down.

"Murder holes," Shawny answered to the questioning villagers. "You'll understand when the time comes."

As they built the defenses, Crafter sent villagers out through their underground minecart system, relaying the defensive plans to all the other villagers all across Minecraft. This was not just a battle for this village, it was a battle for all villages. It was important in Shawny's plans that the monsters be denied any victims from now on, their craving for XP heightened and magnified.

"But why make them crave more XP," the Mayor asked. "It will just make them more violent, more aggressive."

"That's true," Shawny said as he directed the placement of walls, purposely only one block thick at certain locations, "but an angry opponent can be easily manipulated into a position that is favorable for you, and deadly to them. We need to be able to herd *all* of the monsters on this server to one location where they can be trapped. The only way we can do that is to deny them XP from the villages, but offer it to them in a place of our choosing. Then we'll close our trap and get rid of them all in one stroke. But first, we need to survive tonight."

The village slowly changed its appearance throughout the day, from a peaceful collection of buildings clustered around fields of crops, to one of walls and towers ringing the community, some meant to keep monsters out while others meant to keep them in. Gameknight stood atop the tallest tower, a new addition, the stone spire stretching up at least forty blocks into the air, giving him a clear view of the surroundings. He could see activity at the edge of the forest, something moving in the shadows. It looked like an endermen, but this one was somehow different, colored a dark dark red, like the color of blood at sunset, or the color of a nightmare. He could clearly tell it was an endermen as it teleported from the forest edge to the open plain, standing in plain view, a cloud of purple particles forming a haze around the dark creature.

Moving to the ladder, Gameknight slid down to the ground and sprinted through the open gates that now protected the village, ready to face this menace. Running around obstacles and traps, Gameknight ran outside of the village's defenses, coming to a stop and stood out in the open, letting the endermen know that he was here, ready. But the endermen didn't approach, it just watched, then teleported to another location around the village, and then another and another, and watched, surveying their preparations.

Suddenly, a presence moved next to him. Gameknight jumped in surprise, drawing his sword in a single fluid motion, ready for battle and turned towards the new threat.

"Put down your sword, Gameknight, it is only me," said an old scratchy voice; it was Crafter.

"You scared me," he said as he put away his iron sword. He turned away from Crafter and looked back towards the endermen. "Who is that?"

"Ahh, the endermen leader," Crafter said. "He calls himself Erebus."

"What is he doing?"

Erebus disappeared in a cloud of glowing purple sparks and reappeared on the other side of the village, then flashed to a new position, and then another, looking at the new defenses from every angle.

"He's likely mapping out our defenses," Crafter explained, careful to not look directly at the dark monster for fear of provoking him.

Just then, Shawny joined the two of them.

"Shawny, the endermen, he's checking out our defenses," Gameknight said, then turned back to Crafter. "What did you say his name was?"

"Erebus."

"Yeah, Erebus," he continued, talking to his friend, "he can see where the walls are thinner, where they are weakly defended. We need to strengthen the defenses at some of those locations around the village."

"Don't worry, Gameknight," Shawny explained. "We want him to see those places."

"I don't understand."

"Nor do I," Crafter added. "Don't we want to strengthen all places around the village?"

"A flood is coming, my friends," Shawny said, a ring of confidence to his voice. "We cannot stand rigid against this flood for it will wash us away. Instead, we will redirect the flow to where we need it and where we are prepared. All is as it should be; we are ready."

"What of the other villages?" Gameknight asked.

"Word has returned through the minecart network," Crafter said. "The other villages are as prepared as we are. Tonight, this will either be the greatest victory or the end of this server and all creatures living on it."

Gameknight put a reassuring hand on the old NPC's shoulder.

"All will be well, Crafter," Gameknight said, trying to sound confident. "No matter how this ends, we will put up a fight that will be legendary."

"And soon," Shawny added, pointing to the sun.

The square yellow disk of the sun was just starting to kiss the horizon, the sky around it turning a deep red, square boxy clouds glowing white then fading to darkness as the sun descended, the sky filling with stars.

"Quick, back behind the defenses," Shawny commanded.

The three of them sprinted back towards the village, crossing the wooden bridge that spanned the moat that surrounded their village. As they crossed, Shawny broke the wooden blocks, allowing water to fill in. Passing through the gate that was composed of two iron doors, they entered the village, a sea of scared faces looking towards them. The sky darkened and stars began to show their sparkling faces as the defenders moved to their positions.

"Here they come," yelled someone from the tallest tower.

Gameknight climbed to the top of their dirt wall. He could see shapes moving amidst the trees, dark shapes, angry shapes. The torches that had been placed out near the edge of the forest allowed him to see the approaching mobs as they moved through the circle of light being cast on the ground. As first, only a few monsters came out of the dark forest, but then their numbers swelled as they rushed forward, a wave of monsters flowing across the landscape like an unstoppable tide.

"Remember, don't shoot the endermen," Gameknight yelled to the defenders. "If we don't provoke them, they can't join the fight, so archers . . . aim carefully."

He looked about the village, the NPCs looking up to him like he was already some kind of hero. What a joke; a hero, Gameknight999. He was anything but a hero; a gamer that always played for himself and only himself, his only friend, Shawny, here at his side. The responsibility that had been heaped on him seemed to weigh a million tons; all of these lives relying on him. This was crazy.

Well, real or not, dream or reality, he was here right now, and for the first time he would try to help someone else, these NPCs, no, these people. He'd fight to save them, and die if necessary to save them. A shudder snaked down his spine followed by goosebumps that chilled his skin. He was ready.

"Everyone, stand your ground and show no fear," Gameknight yelled to the villagers. "This is your town and your server. We won't let these mobs take it from you." He held his iron sword up high and then stared out at the approaching mobs. "Come on, let's dance."

CHAPTER 10 – Surprise for the Mobs

Instead of all the monsters just rushing towards the village, they came in carefully orchestrated waves. First were the creepers, their four little feet moving in a blur of green and black. They scurried across the plain and approached the village, their dark eyes glaring hatefully at those that stood on the walls, bows in hand. Some fired arrows while the creepers were still far away.

"Hold your fire until they are close enough to hit," Shawny commanded. "Wait until they are in the moat."

The wave of creepers crashed forward, the monsters speeding across the open, grassy plains, then slowing as they waded through the moat that encircled the village. When the first of the creepers hit watery obstacle the archers opened up, their bows casting a rain of iron barbed drops that fell on the monsters with lethal fury. The green creatures flashed red as they were pierced by the projectiles. Some of them died in a liquid grave while others detonated in frustration. Explosions sounded around the village, the creatures blowing up their comrades in chain reactions that did more damage to the carefully constructed moat than to the defended walls. Firing as fast as they could, the villagers pumped more arrows into the green beasts as wave after wave of them attacked specific spots on the wall. More explosions tore at moat, transforming it from a strategically constructed obstacle, to a gaping gash torn into the flesh of Minecraft; the defenders remaining untouched. A cheer rang out across the village as the creepers continued to detonate harmlessly out of reach. Finally, the creepers stopped their advance and stood out of bow shot, waiting. Now the zombies and spiders started their assault, followed by the skeletons.

"Get ready by the gates," Shawny yelled. "Prepare the redstone."

One of the villagers disappeared into a nearby structure, a stone building built on the last day, thick walls and iron barred windows designed to survive creeper explosions and zombie attacks. Inside the room were various switches, each connected to a redstone circuit that controlled the village's defenses.

The spiders and zombies approached the main gate, but also stopped just out of bow range. They'd have to cross the moat, like the creepers, and knew they would get torn to shreds by the archers. And so they waited.

"What are they waiting for?" asked one of the villagers.

"Just wait for it," commanded Shawny.

Suddenly four endermen teleported next to the moat with dirt blocks in their hands, a purple mist floating around each. They placed the brown, spotted blocks into the moat, filling the watery passage with dirt. And then another wave of endermen appeared just as the first teleported away, filling in more of the moat until a solid bridge had been formed, cutting the moat into two. Now the zombies and spiders charged the iron doors, their forlorn moans and staccato clicking filled the air. Just as the surging wave of hatred reached the village's wall, the skeletons stepped forward and started shooting from their side of the moat, firing on the archers that stood atop the barricade. Green clawed fists pounded on the metal doors that protected the village, their frames ringing with the blows, booming like distant thunder. But then suddenly more endermen appeared, their long arms grabbing the dirt blocks into which the doors were attached, then teleported away, carrying with them the critical blocks. Without the supporting blocks, the doors fell to the ground, falling at the feet of the waiting mob; the village was now open.

"Our defenses have been breached," Gameknight yelled. "Everyone draw swords and attack."

"NO," Shawny commanded. "Hold your positions. Let them in."

"What?" Gameknight said, confusion on his face.

"Watch and learn," his friend said proudly as he signaled the villager in the control room.

The monsters flowed into the wall-ringed village, but just as they entered, the red stone switch was thrown. Sticky pistons buried underground all moved as one, opening a wide two-block deep channel before the attacking mob. As the monsters charged, they fell into the trough, the depth of the hole keeping them trapped. Underground, in a tunnel that ran next to the trough, villagers hacked at the monster's feet, the passage letting the defenders rain blow after blow at the exposed legs from relative safety, only the spiders able to hit back, the zombies and skeletons helpless. The villagers made quick work of these monsters, slashing at them as fast as possible while the creatures struggled to escape the murder holes.

Gameknight sprinted across the murder holes and hacked at zombies and spiders, his iron sword flashing like a bolt of lightning, carving great, sweeping paths of destruction through the mobs. He could feel blows landing on him, but his armor was holding up. Like he'd learned in Wing Commander, Gameknight ran from target to target, not stopping to slug it out, but rather used hit-and-run tactics, as he'd taught the villagers, their numbers now joining the battle.

Defenders now stood amidst the attackers, their armored forms moving from zombie to zombie, slashing at furry spiders and pale white skeletons. Amidst the chaos, he saw armored zombies slashing at the defenders, their golden swords wreaking havoc. Sprinting to the beasts, he struck at them from behind, wearing down their golden armor until it fell away, then quickly destroying the monster within, their golden swords, some calling them butter swords, falling to the ground. Nearby villagers snatched up the shiny weapons and turned them on the mobs, carving great arcs of death through the masses. The battle was terrible, with three to four monsters falling for every villager death, the NPCs fighting with a vengeance, trying to push the monsters out of their village knowing full well that their children lay hidden in their homes behind them, terrified, waiting. Gameknight could hear the screams of the dying, the anguish of the NPCs hammering away at his soul, but he had to keep focused. More monsters continued to flow through the breached gate, their numbers beginning to spread out through the village.

"Second redstone, NOW," Shawny yelled.

Another switch was thrown from inside the control structure. Suddenly, walls pushed up from underground, separating the attackers into three groups, stopping them from spreading out, keeping them clumped together.

"Archers, now!"

Villagers suddenly appeared at the top of small towers only five to six blocks high that were positioned throughout the village. They rained pointed streaking death down onto monsters, their stubby arms drawing the bows as fast as they could. The monsters were forced so close together that the archers didn't really even to aim, just shoot into the cluster of hateful beasts. But then a wave of skeletons entered the village, their arrows seeking out archers on towers. Having to duck behind stone blocks for protection, the archers slowed their attack. Gameknight saw the tide of battle starting to shift, the skeletons much better shots than his villagers. Moving quickly, he dove into the cluster of monsters, seeking out the pale, boney creatures.

"Infantry, concentrate on the skeletons," Gameknight yelled as he stormed into the fray.

Again, Gameknight was a killing machine, his sword flowing through the air in great sweeping arcs, hitting more than one target with a single slice. He hacked at the skeletons, ignoring the arrows that now stuck out of his armor, his back looking almost like a porcupine's. More villagers joined the attack, driving at the skeletons, the screams of the wounded, both NPC and mob, filling Gameknight's ears with horror, but he kept on hacking, his only purpose right now, to destroy. But then, he could see a massive group of creepers approaching, followed by large green slimes, their bouncing bodies moving across the plain towards the fallen gate.

"Shawny, the creepers," Gameknight yelled, pointing across the filled in moat.

"I see them," he replied. "Get ready with redstone switch three. Everybody fall back to the inner wall. FALL BACK."

Gameknight hacked his way back to his own lines, attacking targets of opportunity as he sped by. Looking out across the battlefield, he saw the villagers struggling hand to hand with zombies, their swords slashing out to surprise the monsters, the mobs not accustomed to NPCs fighting back.

"Come on, fall back," Gameknight yelled, helping one defender to his feet, then covering his retreat by killing a zombie, then a giant spider.

The NPCs withdrew deeper into the village, moving behind another stone wall, small two block high apertures left open until all had retreated, then the openings were filled in with stone. Gameknight climbed up a set of steps and stood atop the inner wall, seeing the massive wave of creepers approaching. They didn't notice that the ground was composed of grey-spotted gravel instead of the normal brown dirt, they just charged forward, their thirst to destroy overwhelming.

"Wait for it," Shawny yelled.

The monsters now slowed and moved closer to the stone wall, but cautiously, silent commands flowing to them from the endermen, somehow. Erebus suddenly appeared atop the outer wall, looking down at his troops, a look of satisfaction on his face. It looked as if his troops would soon overwhelm this last wall, his creepers taking it down with their explosive lives, the skeletons and zombies flowing in to finish off the survivors. The dark red endermen looked across the village directly at Gameknight and pointed with his long dark arm.

"You have interfered with something that does not concern you, User-that-is-not-a-user," Erebus screeched in a high pitched voice. "Now witness your failure . . . ready . . ."

Before Erebus could give the command to attack, Shawny yelled, "Red stone three, NOW!"

And in an instant, sticky redstone pistons moved underground, removing blocks from under the gravel, and then gravity took over. The gravel fell straight down into a huge torch-lit cavern that has been carved out from under the village, the bottom filled with water four blocks deep. Unable to swim, the mobs sank quickly; their bodies flashing red as they struggled for oxygen, then bobbed to the surface for another gulp of air, then sank again, flashing red again, the creepers dying first. Slowly, the monsters perished, swimming not their strength. In a few minutes, only a few remained, most of them clumped close together, finding purchase near the walls. Village archers struck out at the remaining zombies and spiders as they tried to flee the village, only to find that pistons near the gates had raised, ensnaring them within the village walls, the hunters becoming the hunted. Now trapped between opposing rows of archers, monsters screamed in rage as the defenders fired volley after volley of deadly projectiles, the cross-fire of iron-tipped arrows slicing them to bits in mere minutes.

The monsters were defeated.

A cheer bubbled up from the villagers, first in disbelief, but then as a thunderous chorus of victory and joy. They had survived probably the worst attack ever seen on this server if not in Minecraft history. Gameknight pulled out his pick and quickly carved a hole in the wall and walked out to face Erebus.

The endermen quickly disappeared from the outer wall and reappeared right next to him. Gameknight looked down, holding up an arm to halt any archers from firing.

"You think you won, User-that-is-not-a-user?" Erebus shrieked, venomous hatred in his voice. "This is just the first battle of many. You have protected this village, but there are many villages on this server with much XP to be had. It is just a question of time until this village and all villages are destroyed. And then I'll come for you."

"Big talk coming from the loser," Gameknight mocked. "I think you'll find that the villagers on this server, *all* of them, are not so helpless anymore. Now why don't you go run back into the shadows and stay there where you belong . . . or maybe thirty archers will use you for target practice. You think you can teleport away faster than I can signal them to fire?"

The endermen chief suddenly disappeared and teleported outside the village wall, a look of unbridled hatred on its dark face.

"This isn't over," Erebus screeched. "A storm is coming to cleanse this server and all servers, clearing out the infestation that is NPCs and users. We will flow through these electronic servers and into the physical world until we rule everything."

"Yeah, whatever," Gameknight said as disrespectfully as he could muster. "Don't let the door hit you in the butt on your way out."

And at that, Gameknight999 turned his back on Erebus and sheathed his sword, then held his fist up high and cheered, the villagers joining in. Shawny moved to his side and patted his friend on the back.

"I'm not quite used to seeing you act like a real leader," Shawny said sarcastically. "It's almost like you really care about these NPCs."

Gameknight shrugged as he cast his gaze across the survivors, priding swelling within him. He'd done it, he'd won, but he knew that this was just a battle, and the war waged on, the real battle, the deciding battle yet to come.

CHAPTER 11 – The Plan

The sun rose majestically to the east, bathing the landscape with a golden yellow glow that turned the sky from its terrifying midnight black to warm mixture of orange and red until a cobalt blue flowed across the heavens from horizon to horizon; the terrifying night was finally over. As Gameknight999 watched the sunrise he could hear a bustle of activity as the villagers started reassembling their village, replacing blocks to walls, patching together buildings that had fallen prey to the relentless wave of creepers and resetting redstone traps. The Mayor was at the heart of the activity, wanting his village in shape before the next sunset; he knew the mobs would be back.

"Quickly, let's get everything back into shape," the Mayor yelled. "Send out messengers to the other villages. We need to know how the others fared."

Crafter walked up to Gameknight, who was still looking to the East, lost in thought.

"What now?" Crafter asked.

"This was just the beginning, but they'll be back," Gameknight said softly, motioning Shawny and the Mayor to stand near. "Erebus will return with more monsters, and he won't quit until he levels this village and all the rest on this server."

"This is a war of attrition," Shawny added. "He'll just keep chipping away at the villages until they all fall. Fortifying the villages was smart, but it's not the answer."

Gameknight thought for a minute. He could feel the answer in the back of his mind, but it was illusive, flitting between memories of battle and memories of his old life in the physical world. And then the image of him playing with his three cats, Max, Baxter and Shadow popped in his head. He used to love taunting them with his dad's laser pointer, directing the red spot on the ground and making them chase it throughout the house, but his favorite game was trying to herd all three of them into tight spots, using the laser as bait. It was always challenging, but his greatest victory was getting all three of them to climb into an empty box, all at the same time, the three felines hungry to catch the only thing that mattered to their furry little minds – catching that spot. That's what he needed here, bait.

"Ok, here's the plan," Gameknight said confidently, the solution now clear in his mind. "First of all, we have to deny the mobs any victory. We can't let the villages slowly get whittled down to nothing." Turning to the Mayor, he continued. "Send out messengers to all the villages. Find out which ones took the most damage, and abandon them, distributing the NPCs to the other villagers, boosting their numbers. As villages take damage, we move the people to stronger locations, keeping up the number of people in the surviving villages, so that they can mount a strong defense."

The Mayor looked to one of the villagers that had been listening nearby and nodded his head. Moving quickly, he ran to a cluster of other crafters and relayed the plan, the group then heading to the tall stone tower, the minecart system underground their destination. The Mayor then looked back to Gameknight.

"It's started. It will be done."

"Good," Gameknight said. "We have to deny the monsters any victims, any XP. They have to be hungry, really hungry for something to kill."

"But how will that help us?" Shawny asked. "It will only make them fight harder. I don't see how this helps us."

"You see, if we stop the monsters from killing anyone in the villages, then they will go crazy when the sense someone out in the open," Gameknight explained.

"You mean the other users?" Crafter asked with a gravelly voice.

"Yes, but not just any user . . . me." Gameknight paused to let that sink in, then continued. "I will be the bait that will draw them away from the villages and to a place where we, the users, have the advantage. That's where the final battle for this server will take place."

"This sounds insane," Shawny cried. "You don't know what will happen if you get killed here on this server."

"That's right," Gameknight agreed, "but that's also true for the villagers as well. Life inside the Minecraft software is uncertain. We don't understand it, just like we don't understand life in the physical world, but we continue to live our lives, regardless. I've come to realize that life is a gift, whether physical or digital, and we have to protect this gift with any means at our disposal, and that means me luring the mobs, not just the ones near this village, but all the mobs on this server into a trap that will destroy them all, forever."

"That is indeed a noble quest," Crafter said as he put a blocky hand onto Gameknight's shoulder. "But how do we do it. How will we destroy them all when we get them together?"

"We'll do what we do best," Gameknight999 said proudly. "We'll grief them."

Shawny smiled, understanding.

"Now here's what we'll do."

Gameknight pulled them into a tight circle and explained his plan, laying out the intricate pieces of the puzzle, hoping they would all fit together when the time came. Shawny nodded when it came to his part in this deadly play, his mind already whirling with strategic ideas that would be lethal to the mobs, Crafter and the Mayor accepting their parts as well. Once he'd explained his plan, his three conspirators stepped back and nodded, each seeing the risk in what they were to do, but also seeing the possibility of victory if all went well.

"It's vital that the villages hold out," Gameknight said. "We have to deny the mobs any XP so that they'll chase me across the landscape and into our trap. None can be left behind."

"The villagers will hold out," the Mayor said proudly. "We'll see to that."

"Excellent," Gameknight replied. "Then let's get everything ready. I'll need supplies, weapons and some new armor. Shawny, you'll need lots of tools and food for everyone. After you find the place . . ."

"Don't worry," Shawny interrupted, "I know what to do. You bring the monsters to me and I'll do the rest."

Gameknight999 nodded to his friend, realizing how important his friendship was to him; a thing that seemed a rarity these days. And then Shawny disappeared, a subtle popping sound filling the space where he had been standing, the headband on his ninja skin seeming to be the last to fade away. He was gone.

"You have a stout friend there," Crafter said in his scratchy, aged voice. "Not everyone is blessed with such friendships. You must be a worthy friend yourself."

Gameknight looked at the Crafter, a flash of anger flowing across his face.

Was he mocking me? Was that sarcasm? Gameknight didn't have lots of friends, in fact, he had very few, with most of the players he'd met on Minecraft having ended up at one time or another as the victim of his griefing or trolling. His goal in the past had always been to play for himself and only himself, and don't worry about what other people need, but Gameknight could now see the destructive nature of this attitude. Griefing other people's creations, destroying buildings, causing servers to lag out and crash, . . . all of these things just served to push people away from him, make others avoid him . . . and for good reason. Why should anyone trust him now? Will anyone be there at this final battle to help him, or will he have to face the hundreds of monsters alone, as would be justified. He sighed.

"Yes, Shawny is a good friend, better than I deserve," Gameknight said with a serious tone. "But enough talk, let's get ready."

"We are ready," Crafter said proudly.

"You have everything I'll need already? How is that possible, we haven't moved?"

"One of my abilities as the village crafter is the ability to communicate to those in the caverns that are crafting for me. As we discussed the plan, I had them start making what I think will be needed."

Crafter reached out with a blocky arm and pointed to three NPCs running towards them, coming from the tall stone tower with its secret shaft leading down into the crafting cavern. They ran up to Gameknight and started leaving objects on the ground, new iron armor, food, two stacks of torches, three iron picks, an iron shovel, an arrow, and a diamond sword . . . A DIAMOND SWORD! Gameknight reached out quickly and grabbed the weapon, its icy blue surface almost glowing.

"Diamond, where did you find diamond?" Gameknight asked.

"There are some about, not many, but some," Crafter explained. "I had some of my miners start some branch mines down near the bedrock. They've been mining while we talked. It's amazing how much can be mined when you have fifteen villagers working on it all at the same time."

"Is it enchanted?" Gameknight asked, noticing the shimmering bluish-purple hue that seemed to dance across the blade and handle.

"Yes," Crafter replied, his scratchy voice resonating with pride. "It has *Knockback II* and *Sharpness III*. It should serve you well."

Gameknight held it up to the sun and admired the razor sharp edge, the enchanted weapon casting a warm cobalt blue light glow on his face. Inspecting every inch of the sword, Gameknight scrutinized it carefully, a smile slowly spreading across his face. This was exactly what he needed.

Looking at the other supplies that hovered near the ground, he noticed a single arrow. Picking it up, he held it before his eyes, confusion replacing the smile.

"Why only one arrow? No bow?"

"A single arrow wouldn't be very useful unless you had a really special bow," Crafter said, a smile on his face causing the ancient brow to wrinkle upward. "Give it to him."

Digger came forward and stood directly in front of him, tension heavy in the air. Gameknight had caused the death of his NPC wife, a testament to his selfish, conceited attitude that he'd had until getting pulled into this world.

"I still don't forgive you for what you did," Digger said with an angry voice. "But today, you saved our village, kept all the children and villagers safe from the mobs; saved my children. You did something that was not for you, was not self-centered and not at the expense of others. Today you did something at the expense of yourself, risking your life to save others, and this I can respect and appreciate."

The villager reached into his inventory and pulled out a shimmering bow.

"You left this in our chest the first time you were here, when you . . ."

"When I griefed the village and caused the death of your wife," Gameknight said solemnly, his head lowered.

Digger nodded, then held out the bow to the User-that-is-not-a-user. Reaching out, Gameknight took it and held it up to his eyes, taking in every aspect of the weapon, his *Punch II, Power III* and *Infinity* enchanted bow, the envy of all.

"I'd forgotten about this," Gameknight said, his voice filled with hope. "My old bow, my old friend." Gameknight looked up at Digger and placed a hand on his shoulder. "This bow may tip the scales, Digger, make the difference between success and disaster . . . thank you."

It was something he wasn't used to saying; the words feeling strange in his mouth.

Digger bowed his head.

"It looks like we have everything," Crafter said, his scratchy voice sounding like sand paper scraping against rock. "It's time for us to go."

"Us?" Gameknight999 asked. "What are you talking about?"

"I'm going with you," Crafter said, his voice suddenly sounding clear. "I'm seeing this through to the end."

"You can't," Gameknight complained, his voice growing louder. "The most likely outcome here will be death, and you can't respawn like the users do."

"And you can?" the old NPC asked, his voice resonating like a bell, confidence in their task and clarity in his purpose ringing clear.

Nearby villagers could now hear what was being discussed and were drawing near, uncertainty painted on their faces.

"I don't know what will happen to me," Gameknight stated, "but I do know what will happen to you if you're killed, you'll . . ."

"I've lived a long life, probably longer than anyone else in this world. I've seen many things in my days, more

sunrises that I can count, the deaths of too many friends . . .
too many . . ." Crafter was suddenly lost in thought,
memories of the deceased haunting him for an instant.
"No, my time is done here. It is time I moved on and name
a new village Crafter."

Gameknight999 glared at Crafter, hoping the force of
his will could make the old NPC to back down, but no,
Crafter only glared back, daring him to challenge his
decision. I can't be responsible for this, Gameknight
thought, not another life. He could feel the weight of this
responsibility starting to press down on him, crushing him
like a mighty vise.

The villagers now congregated around the two, all of
them completely silent, eyes locked on the Crafter and the
User-that-is-not-a-user. The tension between the two of
them seemed to almost make the air shake with fear, the
magnitude of what was happening clear to all. And then a
small voice percolated up through the silent crowd, that of
the brave young girl who had first spoken to Gameknight a
day ago, though it seemed like an eternity ago.

"I'll miss you Crafter," she squeaked, her voice shaking
with fear. "You've been good to me, and I will never
forget you."

"I'll always remember your fireworks," said another
voice. "The yellow stars were always my favorite."

"Yes, and . . ."

"I remember . . ."

"Thank you for . . ."

"Fare well . . ."

And then it was a flood of goodbyes, the village having
made the decision for the both of them. The NPCs shared
with Crafter the small moments when he'd touch each and
every life, done some small thing that eased someone's
worries, or made them smile, or saved a life; it was an
affirmation for his existence, a confirmation of his value
and worth in this electronic world, and to Gameknight's

surprise, he saw a square blocky tear flow down the old NPC's face, a smile rising up to meet the salty flow.

The villagers all crowed in to touch Crafter one last time, then moved back to their work, preparing the village for the next attack, likely coming in two days.

"Digger, please stay," Crafter said as he wiped the square tear from his face.

Digger paused and turned around, confusion on his face.

Crafter approached the NPC and held out his own crafting bench, waiting for it to be accepted. Digger took an uncertain step forward, then another and another until he was almost nose to nose with Crafter, his face showing confusion and fear, his wrinkled unibrow accentuating his uncertainty.

"Digger, I choose you to lead the villagers in this area, to craft those tools and items that the users need throughout this land," Crafter said, his voice rising in volume so that all in the village could hear. "I choose you to keep the electronic machine that is Minecraft working smoothly and without lag. I name you Crafter."

Pushing his crafting bench forward, he placed it into Digger's hands, the light brown box seeming to glow in the yellow sunlight. When the crafting bench was accepted, Diggers brown coat suddenly turned to a dark black, a long grey stripe running down the center, Crafter's own coat fading to a forest green. And then it was done. The villagers all turned to look at their new Crafter and nodded acceptance as they went back to work, the old Crafter just smiling a huge smile that stretched around his blocky face and curved up to meet his ears.

"Now we can leave," Crafter said as he wiped the last remnants of tears from his face. "Come, Gameknight, we have to find our final battle and save this world from destruction."

"Oh, is that all we have to do," Gameknight replied sarcastically.

"Yep, that's all."

And the two characters walked out of the village and into the unknown, Crafter humming a melodious tune, their path leading towards the final battle that they both could feel just over the horizon. As they walked, they could hear the sounds of work, digging and stacking of blocks, resetting of redstone pistons, and the crafting of new tools coming from behind the village's wall. None of the NPCs watched them recede into the distance, or they would have seen the tall, dark red, lanky shape watching from the shadows of the forest, a dance of purple particles floating about the creature, narrow white eyes glaring at the pair with overwhelming hatred and a desire to kill.

"I will have my revenge," Erebus screeched softly to himself, the anger in his voice making the trees want to lean away from the source of such tremendous malice.

He chuckled a maniacal laugh.

"You can run, User-that-is-not-a-user, but I *will* find you."

And the endermen chief chuckled again as he faded back into the shadows.

CHAPTER 12 – The Hunt

They walked all day, the landscape of Minecraft beautiful, with clusters of tall oak trees nestled amongst rolling hills of grass and flowers, a white capped snow biome far off to their left. It all seemed so tranquil and gorgeous, well, except for the blood thirsty monsters that were roaming the land, looking to feast on the pair's XP. Gameknight led the way, his head on a constant swivel, scanning the terrain for threats, ducking behind trees or crouching behind hills to avoid large groups of monsters, spiders seeming to be everywhere. Crafter hummed his nameless song as he walked, more out of nervousness than anything else, the melody becoming more dissonant when monsters were near. He wasn't sure how it worked, but somehow Gameknight could feel their path, a tingling in his mind that told him where Shawny was preparing for the last battle.

"So Crafter, if Digger is now the new Crafter of the village, what are you?" Gameknight asked.

"I am but a villager, an NPC as you call us," Crafter said. "Notice, my clothes are no longer the traditional black with grey stripe, the uniform of my old position. Digger, I mean, the Crafter now wears those colors." He pulled out a cookie from his inventory and ate it as they walked, slowing down slightly. "I am nobody, just another being in this world."

"Do I still call you Crafter?"

"Titles are unimportant. You can call me anything you want, it is of no concern."

"Well, you're still Crafter to me," Gameknight affirmed.

"Fine."

They continued on in silence as they played the real-life game of hide and seek, the end result deadly for the hiders, them. Pushing their way through a small corpse of trees, the duo stumbled onto the lone spider. Instantly, they fell on the creature, Gameknight's diamond sword flashing through the air in great shimmering arcs, striking out at the eight-legged monster, killing it instead of allowing the beast to escape and report their position to the endermen, to Erebus. This happened three more times, the lone spiders and singular creepers quickly dispatched, one of them they had to chase for a while before catching it. Clearly, Erebus had the creatures out looking to gather information, their position more important right now than their deaths.

Looking up, Gameknight checked the sun. A feeling of dread spread throughout his body when he noticed the square yellow disk start to gently kissing the edge of the world, then gradually began dipping below the horizon, the sky fading from brilliant blue, to a majestic reddish-orange, and then to a final, deadly black.

"We need to find a place to hide," Crafter said nervously, his eyes darting about as darkness closed in around them.

"We'll be OK for a little bit," Gameknight said confidently. "Just have your pick and shovel ready."

"But we need to find somewhere, a cave or cavern or something, a defendable place to hide."

"Don't worry, Crafter, I have that figured out," Gameknight reassured. "Just be ready with your shovel."

Crafter looked up at his companion, confusion showing on his blocky face, his long grey hair flowing down his back. Slowing their progress, they moved carefully through the landscape, now traversing a grassy plane with low rolling hills covered with blue and red flowers, no trees to hide their presence, but still avoiding the mobs, their numbers now having significantly increased. Erebus clearly had them out looking for them, great hordes of spiders and zombies moving in clusters, their eyes pointing in all directions at once. If one of these groups saw them, they would all fall on the pair, with no chance for defense. Choosing to play it safe, Gameknight brought their trek to a halt.

"We'll hold up here," he said to the old NPC.

"What . . . right here?" Crafter asked, confused as he looked about the flat plain.

"Yep, get out your shovel, let's dig."

They dug a hole four blocks deep, going straight down. It was a cardinal rule to never dig straight down in Minecraft, but Gameknight knew that there was little danger of hitting a cavern or lava this close to the surface. Once they had made it down four blocks, they sealed themselves in, with two blocks of dirt above them. Carving out a block next to him, Gameknight placed a torch so that their little hidey-hole had some light. Turning to Crafter, he could see the fear painted across his square face, fear and terror.

"What's wrong?" Gameknight asked.

"They've seen us somehow," he said pointing upward with his shovel.

Straining his ears, Gameknight999 could hear the mobs approaching, the moaning of the zombies, the peculiar clicking sound of the spiders, the bouncing sound of the slimes, and of course the terrible chuckle of the endermen, all of them clustering nearby.

"How did they see us?" Gameknight asked. "We were underground before any were within view?"

"It's your name above your head, they can see it somehow. Quickly, crouch, your name will disappear."

Gameknight crouched down, lowering slightly and making movement difficult. He couldn't tell if it made any difference or not; how he wished he had an x-ray mod right now. As he looked up at their dirt ceiling, Crafter pulled out his shovel and dug down another block under Gameknight and then under himself.

"What are you doing?"

"Shhhh."

Pulling out a block of cobblestone, Crafter placed the stone above their heads, then another, filling in the ceiling, the blotchy overhead surface lit from the warm glow of their lone torch. Gameknight looked to his companion, confused, questions on the tip of his tongue. Before he could ask, Crafter held up a hand, silencing him, then pointed upward. The sounds of zombies could be heard just beyond the rocky barrier, the suffering moans driving icicles of fear into their minds, freezing their courage. Gameknight shuttered, terror bordering on panic pulsing through his veins, the memory of those sharp claws bouncing around in his head, making him want to just dig his way out and run. What good will that stone ceiling do, Gameknight thought, with so many monsters on the other side. Maybe they should have stopped sooner, found a cave or tall tree, or . . . and then a reassuring hand rested on his shoulder, bringing Gameknight's panic under control a little. Turning, he found his friend smiling at him, his long grey hair glowing in the torchlight.

"Endermen can't take cobble, only natural materials like sand or dirt," Crafter explained. "If they find where we are, at least they can't dig us out. It will keep us safe, for a while."

Pulling out his shovel again, Crafter continued to dig around them, creating a one block space on the perimeter of their two block home. As he dug, he filled the empty spaces with more cobblestone until they were completely surrounded, the stone making them feel a little safer, easing their fears, a little. Once this protective layer was complete, Crafter put his shovel away and just listened, the two companions looking up at the ceiling in fear, the sounds of mobs getting louder, then dissipating as the monsters spread out, hunting their prey.

"I think they lost us," Gameknight said.

"Shhh," Crafter said, then moved his head close to Gameknight's ears. "If we can hear them, then they can hear us. You must whisper," the old man whispered.

Gameknight nodded.

The sounds of their pursuit seemed to get fainter for a bit, the mobs moving farther away, but then individual monsters could be heard, the occasional zombie or spider coming near, all moving in a seemingly random manner.

"They don't know where we are," Gameknight999 whispered, a little bit of tension gone from his voice.

"Possibly," Crafter agreed, his scratchy voice barely audible, "but one thing I've learned after all my years in MineCraft – the nights are long. We must still hope for good fortune here; this isn't over yet."

Just then, an explosion tore through the silence, the blast echoing in the distance, likely a creeper, the rumbling boom causing a little bit of dust to fall from their stone ceiling.

"What was that?" the old NPC asked. "What would have made a creeper go off?"

Gameknight was just about to answer when another explosion rocked their chamber, this one a little closer, then another one just barely noticeable in the distance. He knew what was happening and was about to whisper to his companion when an explosion went off nearby, the ground shaking as the blast echoed through their tiny hidey-hole; their walls held.

"That was close," Crafter said, fear painted on his blocky face. "What's happening?"

"It's like in Silent Hunter," Gameknight said.

"What?"

"Silent Hunter, it's a submarine computer game."

"Submarine?" Crafter asked, confused.

"Submarines are boats that go under water," Gameknight explained with a whisper. "They hunt other ships on the surface, and sink them with torpedoes from the depths."

Boom

He paused as another blast reverberated through their little hole, the sound hurting his ears and choking their hidey-hole with dust. Fear rippled along his spine as he waited for the next blast to kill them both. "When a ship thinks a submarine is nearby, they drop depth charges, bombs that explode underwater, to try to sink the sub."

"But how does the ship know where the submarine is at?"

"They don't," Gameknight continued, "so they drop the depth charges everywhere, hoping to get lucky. Using the last known position of the sub, the ships will fan out in all directions and drop their depth charges, hoping to . . ."

BOOM!!!

Another explosion violently shook the ground, rattling the duo within their stone hole, the undulating ground causing Gameknight to bang his head against the cobblestone walls, his head and ears now ringing.

"That was close," Gameknight whispered, pointing up at the ceiling.

Cracks were now visible on the face of one of the stone blocks overhead. Looking to his friend, he saw that Crafter was now starting to shake. ". . . and hope to hit the sub and sink it. That's what they're doing up there . . . blowing up creepers all over the place, hoping to get lucky, and get us."

"They came close on that last one," Crafter said, his body still shaking, his eyes filled with terror. "You think they uncovered that block?"

"Not sure, but if they see it, we know where the next creeper will go off."

Another explosion went off nearby, the ground shaking, more dust falling down to coat their throats and fill their eyes, but not as close as the last. Fear of the next blast overwhelmed the two companions, panic starting to rule their minds. Crafter looked about their little stone room, trying to find a place to run, but there was none. It looked as if the old man wanted to scream, his fright just barely kept in check. Putting an arm on the old NPC's side, Gameknight tried to reassure Crafter while staying crouched, his dark eyes looking up at the old man. Looking down, Crafter saw the strength in Gameknight's eyes, the determination that they would get through this, and started to calm down; panic abated, for the moment.

More blasts rumbled in the distance, creepers giving up their last breaths in hope of killing the only thing with XP out in the open. The two companions did the only thing they could do right now, they waited and listened in their tiny stone submarine, the destroyers overhead exploding their creeper depth charges randomly across the grassy plain, an unquenchable thirst for their deaths bubbling across the surface of Minecraft. This continued throughout the night, the rumbling of explosions echoing throughout the area, Erebus driving his mob to find his quarry. Occasionally, they heard explosions close to them, but for the most part, the storm of hatred and malice that raged above had drifted away, their fear finally beginning to ease.

They'd survived.

Gameknight's legs were getting stiff, still crouching to hide his user moniker from the predators above. He wanted to stand and stretch, but didn't dare. Just then, Crafter pulled out his pick and started digging away at the cracked cobblestone block overhead.

"What are you doing, Crafter?"

"It's morning."

"How do you know?" Gameknight asked.

"All NPCs can feel the sunrise; it's something we learn growing up. We teach all our children how to sense when the sun sets and when the sun rises. If you can't sense that, then sunset means death if you're not prepared. I felt the sunrise. It's time to go."

Crafter dug quickly through the cobblestone blocks overhead, allowing shafts of sunlight to stream into their hidey-hole, the dust that filled the air creating golden shafts of illumination that would have looked beautiful, if they hadn't just survived the worst night of their lives. Carving out steps from the dirt, he climbed out of their hole followed by Gameknight. Once out of their hole, they were shocked at what they saw. The beautiful grassy plane they had left at sunset was now covered with gigantic craters, the skin of Minecraft torn and gouged by the work of the mobs, the hunt for the pair voracious and relentless. As far as they could see, the terrain now resembled the surface of the moon, lifeless and shattered. Blocks of dirt and stone floated everywhere, remnants from the creeper's work, an occasional flower or clump of grass surprisingly undamaged amidst the destruction, but these were few. Most of the landscape was destroyed by the wave of violence that had crashed over the plain, no man's land from the war to end all wars redrawn here, ninety-five years later, in Minecraft. Gameknight looked to the east and could see the glowing square face of the sun rising over the horizon, its lifesaving presence bathing them with light and warmth.

"Come on, we need to get going," Crafter said.

Pulling out a piece of melon, Gameknight ate quickly, then gobbled down more until his hunger was sated, Crafter doing the same. Drawing his enchanted diamond sword, he started walking, chasing the sun, their destination still tingling in the distance; the location of the final battle. He hoped that Shawny would have it ready, could get other

115

users to help or all was lost. But why would any of the users help him, Gameknight999, the king of the griefers. There probably wasn't a single player on this server that he hadn't done something to, griefed their home, killed them and taken their inventory, . . . Why would they help him, the person that had no friends, only victims. A peculiar sadness swept over him, a feeling that he thought was regret, though he'd never really felt it before. If only he'd been a better friend, a better Minecraft player, if only . . . There was no time for these thoughts right now. He had to protect this world, protect his world, his family, everyone. Squaring his shoulders, he sprinted ahead hearing the reassuring footsteps of Crafter at his side, the old man humming again, but the tune now starting to sound dissonant and filled with fear. With uncertainty and doubt nipping at their courage, the two lone warriors ran on towards their fate.

CHAPTER 13 – Finding the Alamo

The two companions ran across the landscape, relentlessly pursued by the daytime monsters of Minecraft. Spiders seemed to be everywhere throughout the land, the gigantic arachnids seeing them and instantly running away, hoping to give away their position to Erebus. Likely they were being used because zombies were too slow to be of any use for reconnaissance, and creepers, of course, easy to detonate taking with them any useful information they may have gleaned. Using his bow, Gameknight was able to kill the spiders from a distance, something that he was very good at, thought he felt guilty every time he delivered the killing arrow, his skill having been honed at the expense of many a user and NPC. He didn't share his feelings with Crafter but Gameknight suspected that he felt his unease, the old NPC staying conspicuously silent during the long ranged battles, his humming slow to return.

Soon, they left the grassy plains and entered a heavily forested area teeming with life. Packs of wolves could be seen moving about, their white fur standing out against the gnarled bark of the trees.

"Wait a minute," Crafter said as he slowed to a walk.

"Why? We have to keep moving."

"Not yet," Crafter replied.

Reaching into his inventory, he pulled out a stack of bones, remnants of skeletons long dead, and threw them to Gameknight.

"Take some bones," Crafter said, holding one out in his hand. "We need some pets."

"What are you talking about?" Gameknight demanded. "We don't have time for this."

"Yes we do, now just do as I do."

Gameknight picked up the pile of bones and followed Crafter. The old man slowly approached the wolves with bone in hand. Tapping a wolf gently, Gameknight saw red hearts appear above the wolf's head, then a colored band suddenly materializing around the animal's neck. The wolf was suddenly transformed into Crafter's pet.

"Go get some," the NPC said sternly, sounding more like a command than a suggestion.

Shrugging, Gameknight did as instructed, using the bone as a treat for the animals, winning them over as a pet in an instant. In no time, both of them had half a dozen pets following them through the forest, pursuing more as they ran.

"Why did we want the wolves?" Gameknight asked.

"You'll understand soon," Crafter answered. "If you see any more, get them. We'll need as many as we can find."

Gameknight nodded and continued through the dense forest, a circle of furry companions ringing him closely, their occasional barks sounding almost reassuring for some reason. I hope Shawny is ready, Gameknight thought. I hope he can convince the others, or this plan will fail.

Doubt flowed through him with every heartbeat, chipping away at his courage, but then he looked at his companion and felt strengthened. Crafter ran next to him, confident and strong, his long grey hair streaming down his back, courage and determination painted firmly on his blocky face. Turning his head as he ran, the old NPC gave him a smile and patted him on the shoulder, bringing a growl from one of Gameknight's wolves. Throwing the animal a steak, the two continued to sprint, picking up any stray wolves they came across as they plunged through the forest.

Suddenly, a group of six zombies jumped out from behind a thick corpse of trees, all clustered together in the shade of the thick canopy, trying to keep the lethal sun off their backs. Before any of them could attack, the wolves fell on them, snapping at arms and legs with sharp teeth. The wolf pack tore into the green monsters with a vengeance. Bright claws flashed through the air, reaching out for white fur, but the wolves were too fast for the green monsters. The zombies flashed bright red over and over as their HP slowly dropped, sharp teeth tearing at sickly emerald arms. The pack tore into the monsters, white furry missiles diving into the green cluster until the last of the monsters vanished with a quiet pop, leaving behind pieces of floating zombie flesh, and of course XP.

"Now you see why we need the wolves," Crafter said proudly.

Gameknight nodded.

"That was a good idea."

Crafter beamed, then continued to run, his humming lightening their mood a little, the pack following close behind. They sprinted through the dense forest, weaving their way between low hanging leafy branches and past serene pools, their furry protectors falling on zombies and spiders at every opportunity, their destination still drawing them forward towards the distant mountains that occasionally poked their stony face through the forest's canopy.

"I think that's where it's gonna to be at," Gameknight said as they crested a hill, the rocky peak now visible, standing before them tall and majestic, the forest ending at its feet in the distance.

"You think we can make it that far before dark?" Crafter asked, worry creasing his unibrow.

"I feel like we must," Gameknight answered. "Something feels strange, like everything is massing towards this point. I can feel all the anger and violence in this world focused on this spot . . . tonight. We *have* to make it."

Looking over his shoulder, Crafter glanced at the sun, its golden face was just starting to kiss the horizon. He didn't need to look to know how much time they needed; it was just nervousness forcing him to check.

"If we can make it to that next hill in a couple of minutes," the NPC said, "then we should be able to reach the foot of the mountain. I hope your friend has something ready for us, or when we get there we'll find our backs against the mountain and likely surrounded by every monster on this server. I hope he comes through."

"Me too," Gameknight answered, images of zombies storming out of his dad's digitizer and attacking his little sister filling his mind. "Me too."

They sprinted down the hill and bolted towards the next, the sun racing them to the finish line. More monsters started to show their angry faces as they ran, the light level and cover from the trees making it possible for them linger about without bursting into flames. Clawed hands reached out to them, trying to dig into flesh as they sped by. A spider jumped directly into their paths. Gameknight and Crafter hacked at the creature as they jumped over it, the two swords slaying the beast in a heartbeat.

Not stopping to collect the XP, the two companions continued their sprint; the race for their lives. A group of creepers tried to approach them from the right, but their tiny pig-like feet were just too slow, one wolf falling on the mottled green beast, making them detonate, taking the entire group with them; poor wolf, he thought. Not stopping to engage any of the mobs, the two companions just sped through the forest, letting their pack of wolves do their dirty work wherever possible. Gameknight could see a few spiders and zombies run away after seeing them, likely to divulge their location to Erebus, but that didn't matter now, in fact, they wanted Erebus to know where they were and bring his horde. I hope Shawny is ready, Gameknight thought. And then they heard the sound as they started to race up the next hill, the maniacal chuckle of endermen teleporting nearby.

"You hear that," Gameknight said as they ran.

"Yep," Crafter replied stoically. "They're here."

Just then an endermen appeared directly in front of them, its long dark arms down at its sides, purple particles dancing about. Weaving around the shadowy creature, the two quickly looked down and avoided contact, putting away their swords. Endermen can only be provoked into fighting by either attacking them, or looking at them directly in the eyes. Running around another of the shadowy creatures, Gameknight999 and Crafter both knew this well and were careful to look away and not touch the monsters, the nightmares.

The sounds of pursuit were strong behind them, the yelping of their wolves sounding loud at their backs as the mobs fell on their furry protectors. The clicking of spiders and moans of zombies started to get louder until it filled the air as their numbers increased, the rattling of skeleton bones and chuckling endermen adding to the cacophony. The growls of the wolves gradually changed from one of attack, to one of defense, terrified defense, their yelping and screaming accentuating the pain they were likely feeling.

"I hope they just run away," Gameknight said aloud to his friend, the cries of pain filling him with more guilt.

"They won't, unless they get hungry," Crafter answered.

More yelps and canine cries, then nothing from the wolves, just the sounds of monsters; they were alone. Sprinting again, they finally reached the top of the last hill, the rocky mountain standing before them. Stopping for an instant to catch their breath, they looked back towards the forest and were terrified by what they saw. Hundreds, no maybe a thousand monsters were closing in on their position, the angry faces of zombies, skeletons, spiders, slimes, and creepers visible through the tree branches, the occasional endermen just standing . . . watching . . . waiting. It looked like the flow of a massive river, the creatures weaving around tree trunks and over small hills, all focused on their position, on Gameknight999. He could feel their anger, their rage, their desire to kill any and all creatures they encounter.

Gameknight shuttered and shook with fear.

"Come on, we have to get off this hill before we're surrounded," Crafter said, grabbing his hand and pulling him forward.

Gameknight started to run, then sprinted down the hill towards their goal, though he wasn't sure exactly where they were heading. Suddenly, a torch flared to life at the base of the mountain, a sign just barely visible under the glowing circle of light, a steel door under the sign shining bright.

"There, you see it?" Gameknight yelled, the sounds of pursuit getting louder.

Crafter nodded.

The moaning of zombies and the agitated clicking of spiders started to surround them from three sides, the mass of blood thirsty creatures slowly closing in. Looking over his shoulder, Gameknight could see the wave of monsters cresting the hill, the black eyes of the zombies seeming to glow with hunger, the red eyes of the spiders doing the same. They were all focused on Gameknight999. Some of the zombies tumbled down the hill in their haste as they spilled over the summit to reach the User-that-is-not-a-user, the spiders climbing over the green bodies without a thought, their hatred focused on their target.

Shivering with fear, Gameknight pushed on, focused on the torch and doors, salvation waiting for them. As they ran, they could see arrows flying overhead landing in the ground near their path; skeletons firing at them.

"Weave around," Gameknight said, "run a zigzag pattern."

The two ran to the left and right, making them harder to hit. Arrows flew in all directions, but most stuck to the ground near their feet, the occasional barbed point slightly nicking an arm or shoulder. Running zigzag kept the arrows at bay, but allowed the other monsters to catch up a little, slowly closing the distance, the hungry growls getting louder. Would they make it in time? Off to the left, Gameknight could see a cluster of spiders closing in on them, no, not spiders, cave spiders . . . oh no. Milk, they didn't have any milk. How could they fight cave spiders, their poison would certainly get them, milk being the only antidote. Another cluster of cave spiders appeared to the right, farther away than the first, but still effectively boxing them in.

The torch was getting closer; they had to make it. Sprinting as fast as they could, the two friends crossed the last bit of ground as deadly iron-tipped rain sprinkled down on them from the skeletons, the growling sound of monsters at their backs getting louder, angrier.

The duo finally reached the iron doors only to find no switch or button, no pressure plate or means of opening their escape route; they were trapped. Turning to look at the sign, Gameknight saw what was written in large, capital letters; THE ALAMO. It was a joke from Shawny; the last stand of the Texan army facing off against the Mexican army, the famous battle now being relived here in Minecraft, unfortunately they were playing the part of the Texans, and that historic battle didn't end very well for the defenders.

Crafter banged on the iron door with his fist, yelling to be let in. As he yelled, Gameknight turned and faced their pursuers. The monsters had stopped running and were slowly approaching, apparently wanting to revel in the moment of destroying the last user in this world. Gameknight could see endermen standing at the back, just watching, a cloud of purple forming a colored haze around the dark creatures. Then a new endermen appeared amidst the mob, this one a little taller than the rest, colored a dark crimson instead of the characteristic black; Erebus, his eyes blazing. Gameknight could hear Erebus chuckle in the distance, then his maniacal voice rose above the din of the mobs, uttering a single word, the word all the monsters waited to hear.

"ATTACK!"

And the monsters charged forward, a thirst for death filling their eyes, and all Crafter and Gameknight999 could do was draw their swords and wait.

CHAPTER 14 – The Bait

Suddenly, the iron door opened and a familiar face appeared peeking out smiling a mischievous grin, Shawny.

"Hi there," he said playfully. "You wanna come in or what?"

"Shawny!" Gameknight yelled, then grabbed Crafter and pulled him inside, the iron door slamming shut behind them.

This triggered a burst of activity outside, moans and growls of frustration and hatred. Pounding instantly commenced as the zombies reached the door, their blunt fists trying to smash in the iron barrier.

"Where have you been?" Gameknight asked as he backed away from the door, moving farther into the tunnel.

"I've been here," Shawny answered. "Just waiting until you had the monsters all riled up. We need them nice and angry for this thing to work."

"Is everything prepared?" Crafter panted as he tried to catch his breath, sweat beaded on his face.

"Of course," Shawny replied. "But it wasn't easy getting some of the users to help. You've pissed off a lot of people, Gameknight. You don't have a lot of fans."

Gameknight looked to the ground, ashamed of his behavior for maybe the first time in his life. Looking up at his friend, maybe his only friend, he was grateful that he was here. Glancing up at the ceiling, Gameknight noticed the shining silvery thread that stretched up from Shawny's head and through the rocky ceiling, connecting him to the server, his name floating overhead suspended on nothing, but glowing bright in the dimly lit tunnel.

"I know," he said solemnly. "I wasn't very nice to other people."

"Not very nice?" Shawny said, laughing. "You were a complete jerk."

"Yeah, I know. I was disrespectful and offensive, and hurt other people for my own enjoyment. I was out for myself and only myself." He sighed. "It's a wonder anyone would even come to help me after the way I treated everyone . . . even you Shawny. Thank you."

Shawny looked at Gameknight with a curious look.

"I never thought I'd see day," Shawny said, a smile growing on his face.

"What?" Gameknight asked.

"You saying thank you," his friend replied.

Gameknight patted his friend on the back, but was quickly brought back to reality as the sound of endermen at the door echoed through the passage.

"Come on," Shawny said. "We need to get to the cavern before they break through. The endermen will quickly take away the blocks of dirt around the doors, and then they'll be in."

Shawny led the pair deeper into the passageway, torches placed sparingly in the walls to provide some light. It slowly led downhill, deeper underground, curving this way and that, the tunnel cooling as it descended. At times it was two to three blocks wide, at others only a single block, forcing the group to follow single file.

"You need to know something," Shawny said in an unusually serious tone as they ran through the tunnel. "Something is wrong with Minecraft."

"What do you mean?" Gameknight asked.

"Respawning is messed up somehow."

"Respawning?"

"When we die, we don't respawn," Shawny explained. "We just get kicked off the server and can't reconnect, like we've been cut off or banned, but not just on this server, on all servers. Our Minecraft gets corrupted, somehow and won't connect. All the other users on the internet are talking about it."

"Does the screen mention the ban hammer?" Gameknight asked.

"No, we just can't connect to anything. The servers show in our server list, but we can't get to any of them. All of these users here know this; if they die here, they won't ever be able to get back into Minecraft. If we all die, then you'll be on your own."

"That's encouraging," Gameknight said sarcastically as they moved quickly through the tunnels.

"It's the war," Crafter interjected, as they moved through the tunnels, the sounds of monsters in the distance adding a little haste to the journey. "The mobs have taken enough XP to destabilize this world, changing the mechanisms that control this server. They're getting ready to move up to the next server plane, closer to the Source. They need this battle to destroy this server and move up to the next level."

"What happens if *you* die?" Shawny asked his friend, concern in his voice.

"I don't know, but it hurts . . ." Gameknight paused for a moment as the memories from that first spider flooded his mind. "It hurts to get hit by the mobs, hurts like it's for real. I don't think I want to know what it feels like to die; it's likely unpleasant to say the least. What I'm afraid of, is will I respawn, or maybe get kicked from the game and end up back in my basement, or . . ."

"Or what?" Shawny asked in a quiet voice, almost a whisper, the shuffle of their feet filling the tunnel with hushed echoes.

"Or maybe I just die . . . you know . . . for real."

127

Just then, the narrow tunnel ended opening up to a massive cavern filled with lava, an island of stone and sand in the center surrounded by a sea of burning rock, the walls of the cavern formed from dirt and stone. A sulfurous smell filled the chamber, instantly assaulting the senses, the blast of heat from the molten rock hammering the trio in the face, making them take a step back. The size of the place filled Gameknight with awe, the massive island at the center likely able to hold a thousand people, but more impressive was the incredible volume of lava, the lake stretching out deep into the recesses of the cavern, at places flowing out of sight. Roughly hewn walls and ceiling surrounded the lava lake, clearly mined by the users with their pickaxes, the gigantic chamber carved out of the flesh of Minecraft just for this battle. Tunnels could be seen at the back of the cavern, each carved by an army of users, the passages lit with torches. Where they led, Gameknight wasn't sure, but for some reason felt reassured that they were there.

A circle of torches ringed the cavern, each placed four blocks high and spaced five blocks apart but the burning embers offered little light compared to the orange glow of the lava, their existence likely left over from the incredible building process of this massive chamber. A set of stone stairs led down from the narrow tunnel to the cavern floor, the steps leading to a narrow bridge of stone that spanned the boiling lake and led to the huge island in the center. On the other side of the stone island was another bridge, the construction similar to its twin, one bridge to get on the island, and one bridge to get off. All the way on the opposite side of the burning lake was a small ledge maybe ten blocks wide ringing the far side of the lava. The shelf was large enough to hold perhaps a hundred defenders, though currently there were none, now.

"Where is everyone?" Crafter asked, fear in his voice.

"They said they'd be here," Shawny replied, his voice sounding agitated, and a little scared.

The sounds of monsters could be heard in the tunnel behind them. Gameknight could almost feel their malice and hatred for all living things. He was scared.

"Quickly, across the bridge," Shawny said, running across the stone path, lava flowing on either side.

The three companions crossed the stone bridge and reached the large central island. They could feel the heat from the lava as sparks and ash leapt up into the air, the molten rock lighting the chamber as if it were day.

"How are we gonna do this?" Gameknight asked. "We can't hold the bridge with just three of us."

"We don't want to hold the bridge," Shawny explained. "We need to lure them *all* onto this island, then we'll have a little surprise for them."

Just then the sounds of the mobs filled the cavern, the tunnel opening filling with zombies and cave spiders, white skeletons and glowing green slimes showing between the arms and legs of those in front. A chill flowed down Gameknight's spine as fear, no terror filled his soul. There were so many, hundreds, maybe a thousand; how could they do this, how could they survive. If only he hadn't been so selfish, so arrogant and disrespectful, so . . .

Suddenly, a presence appeared next to him, popping into existence noiselessly. It was a user. Gameknight could see letters hovering above his head, a long silvery thread reaching up and piercing the stone ceiling as if it were not there. The letters spelled out Disko42, the famous redstone master. Then another user appeared, another silver thread stretching up into the air, PaulSeerSr. And in an instant, the island was flooded with users appearing from nowhere, each one with sword drawn, many with diamond armor, some shimmering with enchantments, others just dull iron, but all ready for battle. The island was now crowded with probably thirty to forty users, the sudden appearance making the mobs at the tunnel opening stop, their hungry eyes focused on the threats. More people were appearing in the cavern, some adding to their numbers on the island while others appearing on the rocky ledge on the opposite end of the chamber. A look of determination was painted on every face, the users ready for battle.

Gameknight999 looked about him and was stunned at the high level players he saw, AntPoison, SkyKid, HoneyDo, Zefus, Sin, Pips, SgtSprinkles, . . . the most prominent and most skilled players in the game, and they were here to help him; he felt honored.

"Thank you all for coming and helping me out," Gameknight yelled so that all could hear.

Some of the players laughed.

"We aren't here for you, Gameknight," scoffed one voice off to his left.

"Yeah, we're here because of the weird things happening with Minecraft," said another voice.

"And because of Shawny," said AntPoison next to him. "He said this was important and that someone needed our help. He didn't tell us it was the great Gameknight999." Sarcasm dripped from his voice.

A few more grumbles could be heard throughout the crowd, the thought of helping the worst griefer in Minecraft not sitting well.

"Look, the mobs are trying to take over Minecraft and we need to stop them," Gameknight pleaded. "Forget about me, right now we need to save Minecraft or these mobs will break through into the physical world."

Some laughed, but most just stayed silent, glaring at Gameknight999.

"I hear that laughter and see the disbelief in your faces," Crafter snapped, "but there is more at stake here than your silly game." The uses were shocked to hear this NPC speak, and even more surprised to see a sword in his hand. "The NPCs in Minecraft are alive, like me. We are

130

self-aware, know that we exist and feel a sense of self-worth. We have hopes and dreams, and you griefers and trollers think this is just a game and that NPCs are expendable. Well, here's a news flash for you; we feel pain. We feel despair when our wives or children are killed. We feel sadness when our homes are destroyed by your careless use of power. But right now, all the NPCs across this server are fighting the mobs, putting their lives on the line to save this world and yours as well.

"There are servers above this world that are closer to the Source, each level having stronger and stronger mobs, and the zombies, spiders, endermen and creepers want to destroy it all, everything, all the way up to the Source. And when the Source goes, everything goes and the mobs will be released into your world, the physical world." Crafter turned to glare at those on the island, pointing an accusatory finger at the users. "So you keep laughing at me and Gameknight but remember this moment, the time when you had a chance to stand against the flood. But when the creepers come to your house and blow a hole in the wall to let the zombies and spiders come into your bedrooms, you can remember that you had a chance to make a difference, but instead of fighting, you just laughed . . . and in the end, when the black claws of the spiders are shredding through your bed sheets and the zombies are tearing at your flesh, for real, you'll probably hear their moaning laughs. So remember this moment and despair."

"He's right," Shawny said. "I've seen what's going on here, and it's something bigger than just us. We need to stop these mobs right here, and right now, or who knows what will happen."

The users listened to Crafter and Shawny, considering their words, then talked amongst themselves, some of them stopping their debate to glare at Gameknight, then continued to argue, the mobs still holding their position on the other side of the bridge, unsure, waiting. Finally, a voice of reason, HoneyDo, rose above the rest, swaying the users to help, his voice normally sounding funny and silly but the seriousness of his words and the commanding tone in his voice swayed the masses.

"We've talked," said HoneyDo, "and we'll help, but not for him," gesturing to Gameknight, "for Minecraft. We can all tell there's something brewing on the servers, and if this battle with help, then let's get it done."

Gameknight breathed a sigh of relief, knowing that the presence of these users might make the difference, tipping the scales in their favor, hopefully.

"Thank you all," Gameknight said, then turned to face the mobs, sword drawn, ready for battle, but the monsters still remained motionless at the mouth of the cavern, sensing the trap.

"Why won't they attack," Shawny asked.

"They suspect a trap," Crafter whispered. "We have to get them onto this island."

"How?" Honeydo asked. "Maybe we could offer them some Jaffa cakes?" His laughter filled the chamber.

"Get serious," Zefus snapped, giving his friend a shove. "What are we going to do?"

"We have to draw them to us," Crafter said in a low voice, "but how?"

"Like this," Gameknight said as he stepped forward towards the monsters. "EREBUS, SHOW YOURSELF!"

Nothing happened. Gameknight walked across the island and stood near the end of the bridge, the monsters glaring at him from the other side, their moans and growls filling the air.

"EREBUS, SHOW YOURSELF OR BE KNOWN AS THE MOST COWARDLY ENDERMEN IN MINECRAFT!"

This insult caused the zombies to cease their moaning and the slimes to stop their bouncing, all of the mobs shocked at the challenge. Suddenly, a dark red presence appeared at the other end of the stone bridge, a purple haze floating about him; it was Erebus, the leader of the mobs on this server. The endermen glared across the bridge at Gameknight999, its eyes burning white hot with rage. Gameknight quickly looked down.

"What did you say, User-that-is-not-a-user?" Erebus cackled in a high pitched screeching voice. "You want to come over here and talk? Well, come on over."

"I have nothing to say to you, beast, I just pity you and your little pets behind you. Your cowardice will be known across all the servers of Minecraft; a thousand mobs afraid of a few users . . . pathetic."

This brought forth a grumbling from the mobs, the zombies the loudest. A few stepped forward, wanting to attack, but Erebus held out a long arm, holding them in place, his tall dark form blocking the bridge.

"Ha ha ha," Gameknight laughed. "You can't even control your own beasts. I pity you. You were no match for me back at the village, and you're no match for me here. You are wise to stay out of this battle, though your death will be no loss to this world, just another insignificant bug getting squashed."

He could see the endermen start to shake, his eyes now burning red.

"You endermen are nothing but just thieves, taking a block of dirt here, sand there. Is that all you can do, steal. You have no purpose just like your little pets. You are all pathetic, a programming mistake. Well, you can go no further, I forbid it."

Gameknight drew a line on the ground with his diamond sword, a long scratch visible at his feet.

"You have terrorized villages all across this server, taken the lives of NPCs and users for no reason other than to satisfy your thirst for death . . . well, you are now forbidden from causing any more misery. I draw the line, here," Gameknight yelled. "None may pass unless they go through me first, though I doubt any of you are strong enough or brave enough to try."

Erebus was about to burst, now shaking visibly.

Filling his mouth with saliva, Gameknight spit towards the clusters of monsters, a scowl on his face . . . and then he laughed at the mob, a disrespectful, mocking cackle that echoed throughout the chamber.

And that was the last straw. The rusty wire that held the cork that kept all of that anger and rage bottled up in the passageway suddenly broke free. Rushing forward, the mobs charged towards the users with only one thought in mind, kill. Gameknight drew his bow and fired missiles at the oncoming wave of death, killing a zombie, then a cave spider, then a skeleton, and then was pulled back across the island by a set of strong hands, firing as he was dragged away. Turning, he saw Shawny on one side of him, SkyKid on the other. Releasing him, they both drew their swords.

"Remember the plan," Shawny yelled, then turned to face the onslaught that was rushing towards them.

Gameknight notched another arrow, then moved to the front of the group of users, the eyes of a thousand monsters focused on him, and to his surprise, he was not afraid. For the first time, he was doing something to help others instead of himself, and it felt good. He hoped it would still feel good when the mass of fangs and claws started to tear into his flesh. Sighing, Gameknight stood his ground, and waited.

CHAPTER 15 – The Trap

The mobs charged across the stone bridge with only one thought in mind, kill Gameknight999. In their haste to get across, many were pushed off the narrow walkway, falling into the waiting arms of the molten lava that surrounded the bridge and island. It made no difference, though, a handful of monsters killed by their own thirst for violence as compared to the hundreds streaming out of the tunnel; the odds were still impossible.

The defenders opened up with bows, striking out at the monsters from a distance. Gameknight's enchanted weapon with singing as the bow string vibrated after every shot, reverberating with the other bow strings nearby making a sound like an orchestra warming up, every filament oscillating on a different note, both dissonant and harmonious at the same time. He fired a head shot at a zombie, then another one at a cave spider, then a skeleton, his hand not able to draw back the bow fast enough to hit all the targets before him. An arrow bounced off Gameknight's armor, a gift from a skeleton. Brushing it aside, he kept firing.

"Concentrate on the cave spiders," Shawny yelled.

The cave spider's poison was lethal, the only antidote being milk, something that none of them thought to bring to this battle. The smaller cousin of the standard Minecraft spider, they were ferocious in battle, typically found in dungeons underground. Now, they led the charge across the stone bridge, their furry, dark blue bodies scuttling across the ground on eight short, hairy legs. All the bowmen focused their shots on these beasts, firing arrow after arrow at the black furry terrors. In no time, all of the spiders had become pin cushions, feathered spikes sticking out of their bodies, then popped into nonexistence.

Another arrow streaked over his shoulder, striking the user behind him.

"Now, aim for the skeletons," Shawny yelled as the monsters came closer. "Take out their archers."

Some of the zombies were pushing forward, almost in reach of the defenders. Their bows would offer little defense against the green monsters when they were close. Drawing his sword, Gameknight999 charged forward.

"For Minecraft," he yelled, the battle cry resonating off the stone walls of the cavern.

Reaching the first zombie, Gameknight struck out at his head, killing him in three blows. He then turned and sliced at his neighbors, but some of the zombies were trying to get around him, encircle him with their green, extended arms. Suddenly, there were users at his shoulders, Disko42 and PaulSeersSr, each with an enchanted diamond sword in their hands, then Zefus adding to their numbers. Their blades were shimmering cobalt blurs as the came down on their opponents, cleaving zombie bodies into nonexistence, but the mass of attackers was too much for the three defenders to stand their ground.

"We have to pull back," PaulSeersSr yelled.

"No, fight like in Wing Commander," Gameknight said as he slashed at a gold armored zombie, butter armor he remembered someone calling it in a video, "hit and run, hit and run. Come on, follow me."

Gameknight then ran to the left, the three users following. They streaked across the battlefield, striking out at targets of opportunity as they passed, not killing the zombies, just doing damage as they streaked by. After running across the width of the island, they turned around for another pass. This time, their second attack on those at the front of the mob was lethal, their blades killing the zombies, brushing away the leading edge of the monster army like an eraser to a white board, but still the mobs pushed forward, now regular spiders pushing their way to the front, the slower bouncing slimes just starting to make it across the rocky bridge.

"This isn't working," Disko42 said. "We have to get off this island."

"Not yet," Gameknight yelled, slashing at a spider, the furry beast managing to land a blow before disappearing, "we have to get all of them on the island, so that we can spring the trap."

"Then we need to pull back, to make room for them," Zefus said, slashing at a nearby skeleton, changing the creature to a pile of bones after two swings of his shining blade. "Move back to the other bridge."

"Right," Gameknight agreed.

Disengaging from the battle front, he moved back to their archers, Shawny at the front.

"Pull back to the other bridge," he said to his friend. "Have swordsmen go to the front and protect the retreat, archers to the other side of the lava. Get ready with the redstone."

Shawny nodded and gave the commands. Half of the archers quickly filed across the bridge as the other half drew blades and charged forward. Gameknight could see one of the users, Honeydo, move to a lever that was placed on the dirt wall of the cavern, waiting for the signal to throw the switch; the first half of their little surprise.

"Swordsmen, forward," Gameknight yelled, his own glowing sword held up high. "FOR MINECRAFT!!!"

The warriors charged forward, echoing the battle cry. To his surprise, he found Crafter at his side, his own iron sword swinging wildly, cleaving monsters in two.

"What are you doing here," Gameknight yelled. "Get to the other side of the bridge where it's safer."

"Our fates are tied together, my friend," Crafter replied. "I stand with you."

A spider leapt at the duo. Their swords rang together as they simultaneously attacked the furry beast. Sprinting across the battlefield, Crafter and Gameknight were a whirlwind of death, spinning between monsters, one of them attacking while the other defended. It was like watching a graceful ballet, except, of course, for the mass of claws and fangs that were reaching out at them, looking to rend flesh from bone. As they made their second pass, Gameknight noticed that most of the monsters were on the island now except for the creepers, who were staying back, all of them clumped on the bridge at the other side of the cavern, the endermen still in the mouth of the tunnel. Gameknight could feel all of the monster's anger and hatred, their thirst for his death somehow resonating within his mind. It was a terrible feeling, all of that malice focused on him, but he had to shove it aside, throw up some kind of barrier or be overwhelmed. Pushing back his fear, no, terror, he sought out his friend, Shawny, and found him on the right flank, sword flashing through slimes, cutting them in half, then chopping at the smaller green bouncing blobs. Moving to his side, Gameknight pointed at the creepers and then gestured at all the monsters.

"It's time," he yelled to his friend.

Shawny nodded, then turned to Honeydo, ready to give the order, the blocky hand already on the switch. Before Honeydo could move, an endermen appeared at his side, reached out with its long black arms and took the block of dirt on which the lever was placed. The switch fell to the ground along with the redstone that was placed behind it, floating momentarily on the stone, then fell into the lava; the lever was gone. Another endermen appeared to take more dirt blocks, its maniacal chuckle driving spikes of fear into those nearby, then disappeared in a cloud of purple particles, redstone floating on the ground, the piles of red dust bobbing up and down as if floating on ocean swells.

"The redstone," Honeydo yelled to Shawny, his English accent still sounding humorous, even at this moment, "it's destroyed."

Shawny ran across the bridge, pushing through the defending archers on the narrow ledge and stood next to Honeydo. The redstone circuit was completely destroyed.

"Does anyone have any levers?" Shawny yelled.

No one did.

"We have to close off the monster's escape, destroy the far bridge," Shawny said, fear in his voice, "or they'll escape."

They all knew if the monsters escaped, then the battle was for nothing and would have to be replayed again, somewhere else on this server that is if they survived the battle at all.

Running back onto the island, Shawny called to his friend. Disengaging from the battle, Gameknight and Crafter came near, their armor scratched and dented from the blows they had been receiving.

"The redstone trigger for the far bridge is ruined," Shawny explained. "We can't destroy their escape route. The monsters will be able to get away when we trigger the trap; the plan's a failure."

Lowering his gaze, Shawny looked to the ground in defeat, an arrow streaking overhead, just barely missing his helmet. Gameknight glanced at the far bridge, then surveyed the battlefield, the rocky island littered with the armor and weapons of the fallen. The monsters were pushing forward, driving their swordsmen back to their side of the island. Their users were shooting from the narrow ledge, firing arrows as fast as they could, slowly reducing the mob army, but there were so many monsters and so few defenders that it looked as if they had little chance.

"Without destroying that bridge, the plan will never work," Gameknight said solemnly. "You should retreat, take the tunnels out the back of the cavern and run."

The taste of defeat sat bitter in his mouth. They'd lost; he'd lost. This world of Minecraft will be destroyed and these mobs will get closer to the Source, closer to his family, his little sister. What had he done? If only more had come, if only he hadn't been such a jerk to all those other players, maybe . . . maybe . . . and then the sound of Erebus' chilling laugh resonated throughout the chamber. Turning, Gameknight stared across the cavern and locked his eyes with the dark red endermen. The mob king was actually smiling somehow with an eerie, toothy grin, like a snake about to strike, and then Erebus laughed again as all hope left Gameknight999.

CHAPTER 16 – The Meaning of Sacrifice

"NO," Crafter yelled. "There can be no defeat. We don't give up. There are too many people relying on us to protect them." He then raised his voice so that all the defenders could hear. "Defeat is not an option," and then the NPC yelled with a strength that shocked everyone in the chamber, monster and user alike, "MINECRAFT!!!" His battle cry reverberated throughout the chamber like thunder.

And then Crafter did something that no one could believe. The battle actually paused as both attackers and defenders stopped fighting to watch the unbelievable. Crafter sprinted out into the battlefield and crossed the monster crowded island, pushing past giant spiders and shoving aside zombies and slimes to reach the far end. Running through the entire, thousand-strong mob army, he crossed onto the bridge full of creepers, striking out at the green mottled creatures, making one start to hiss and blink, the deadly explosive fuse now lit. He then turned to another and hit that one, starting another walking bomb as well, then another and another until at least half a dozen creeper were blinking, glowing bright. In a burst of sound and flying blocks, the creepers detonated blowing apart the stone bridge and revealing TNT buried underneath which also started to blink, the black and red blocks readying their own explosive gift. The TNT then exploded in an even larger ball of destruction, taking with it the entire bridge and all the occupants standing on top, including Crafter; the rear escape route from the island now destroyed. The monsters were trapped.

"Nooooo," Gameknight screamed as he watched his friend's body fly up into the air surrounded by the glowing balls of XP from the deceased creepers, his armor shredded, his body blinking red with damage.

To Gameknight, it looked like it was happening in slow motion, his friend's body slowly being thrown upward into the air, the glowing balls of XP flowing into him in a whirlwind of color as his grey hair streaming behind him like a silvery flag. With every muscle tensed, his breathing shallow, and his heart pounding away in his chest, Gameknight locked eyes with Crafter as he flew through the air. A look of overwhelming sadness mixed with terror washed over Gameknight's face. His friend, he was dying.

"Crafter," he yelled, his echoing throughout the chamber. "CRAFTER!!!."

And then, Crafter did something that Gameknight would never forget . . . he smiled. A look of satisfaction seemed to wash over the old NPC as his body flashed red over and over again, his health quickly decreasing. Through the crashing wave of sadness, Gameknight understood. Crafter had given his life for those that he loved, his village, friends and loved ones. He'd given the last measure of his life, his last breath in a selfless act that might save all their lives; a spectacular end to a life. As his friends last bit of health ebbed away, Gameknight could tell that he was humming that melodious tune that he always seemed to enjoy, then he closed his eyes and vanished from sight.

Crafter was dead.

Gameknight fell to one knee, overwhelmed with grief. His friend was dead. A pain like nothing he'd ever felt before pulsed through his very soul. Worse than the black claws of the spiders or the razor tipped fingernails of the zombies, this pain encompassed every aspect of his being, his body, mind, and spirit crying out in agony and hopeless despair. His eyes had been locked onto Crafter's as he died, the smile and look of satisfaction on his friend's face something he'd never forget. Why was Crafter smiling? What had he been thinking?

Someone picked Gameknight up and dragged him off the island, he wasn't sure who, as sorrow and grief flowed over him like a terrible storm. He thought it might have been Zefus, or maybe Sin, but he wasn't sure, and didn't care. And then Shawny was at his side.

"Crafter is dead . . . my friend, dead," Gameknight said as he wept, square tears flowing down his face. "Why did he do that? Why did Crafter sacrifice himself like that? He had to know that he wouldn't survive."

"He did that for all of us," Shawny said solemnly. "He did it for everyone on this server, his family, his village . . . he did it for everyone."

"But why? He knew he couldn't survive, knew he'd be killed. How could he do that?" And then understanding burst forth; Crafter had sacrificed himself because of the love he had for his family, his friends, his village . . . Minecraft. He'd willingly sacrificed himself for the ones he cared for, because he held their love so dearly that losing his own life to the explosive tempers of the creepers was a worthy exchange, knowing that he might be saving those that he held most dear. A feeling of pride flowed over Gameknight, knowing that such a noble and brave person had been his friend. Somehow, Gameknight felt stronger and braver with this realization. "I won't let your sacrifice be in vain, Crafter," he said aloud to no one, to everyone. "I won't let you down."

Drawing his shimmering diamond sword, Gameknight stood up and faced their enemies. The mobs were trying to get across the last remaining bridge, swordsmen holding back the vile monsters from on the stone causeway, but just barely. Archers on the narrow ledge that ringed the island were pumping arrows into the beasts, aiming for those that were charging the bridge, lending support to the swordsmen, but they could not hold, the wave of monsters just too great. When one fell, two more took its place, but the users still had one more surprise left in store for the mob.

"Get ready to throw the switch," Shawny yelled over his shoulder.

Gameknight turned and saw AntPoison standing at another redstone lever, his blocky hands ready. Suddenly, an endermen appeared in a purple haze of particles, teleporting from the other side of the cavern. The dark creature pushed AntPoison, shoving the diamond clad user into the lava, then reached out and took the block on which the lever was placed, it too falling into the lava. Users rushed to attack the creature, swords swinging, but the tall monsters just teleported away again, it's maniacal laugh echoing throughout the chamber. Their last trap, last hope, was now destroyed.

"What are we going to do?" Shawny said, his voice shaking with fear.

For the first time, he didn't seem in control, his confidence shattered. This uncertainty quickly spread through the surviving users, all of them eyeing the tunnels at their back that would lead to the surface, to safety, and to defeat. A few started to run away.

"No, we can't retreat," Gameknight yelled. "We have to fight."

"For what?" someone answered. "To get banned from Minecraft forever, when we can just go find a safe place and disconnect."

"Yeah, why should we destroy our own chances to play," another voice complained.

"You don't get it," Gameknight answered, yelling at the top of his voice. "This isn't just a computer app. These people in Minecraft are alive, and have suffered just so that we can play this silly game. Now we have to give back, do something for them instead of for us."

A voice near him laughed.

"Ha ha ha, Gameknight999 doing something for others instead of himself; that's a laugh," SkyKid said, his sword now sheathed as he slowly backed away from the battle towards the escape tunnels at the rear. "Besides, we can't fight that many monsters and survive, it's suicide. We had the trap set, and it didn't work. What are you going to do, magically set it off and destroy all the monsters; how are you gonna do that . . . huh. Are you gonna run out there into that mob of fangs and claws and get torn to bits?"

Silence filled the room, the battle paused to hear the exchange, Erebus now standing at the head of his army, chuckling a spine tingling laugh that only an enderman can make.

"Yes, User-that-is-not-a-user, what *are* you going to do," Erebus said in a shrill, dangerous voice, his eyes burning bright against his dark red face.

Defeat seemed to wrap around him like funeral shroud, the bitter taste filling his soul. He'd failed Crafter, Digger, that little village girl . . . his sister. He'd failed them all. Slowly, Gameknight lowered his head as a feeling of despair flowing over him like a relentless thunderstorm, feelings of abject failure thundering throughout his soul, driving all hope from him. Erebus laughed, the cackle echoing like thunder in the now silent chamber, but then the playful tune that Crafter always seemed to be humming started to percolate up through his memory, pushing away the maniacal laughter. It was a song of happiness, a melody that celebrated the beauty of life and being alive in this wonderful world of Minecraft; it was harmonious joy, and at that instant it filled Gameknight with hope. He now understood his friend, his overwhelming delight at being on this journey, serving his village with his last breath; and then clarity came to Gameknight. Images of Crafter, his joyful smile and love of life floated through his head as he finally understood what he must do, fear and apprehension filling his soul.

Slowly, he put away his sword. Triumphant laughter came from Erebus, then started to erupt from the mobs, a cackling that filled the chamber, making the users shield their ears from the cacophony. Shawny lowered his head as did other users, defeat painted across their faces. Some of them started to move to the escape tunnels, looking for a safe place to disconnect without getting attacked. But to everyone's surprise, Gameknight started to hum a joyful tune, Crafter's song, the harmonious notes cutting through the laughter of the monsters like a blade through butter.

Slowly pulling out his pick, the dull iron tool slightly dented and chipped, almost used up, like himself. Raising his head, Gameknight looked straight into the glowing eyes of Erebus and smiled. The endermen started to shake as the User-that-is-not-a-user's glare started to provoke the dark beast, and then he sprinted for the center of the island. As with Crafter, the mobs were shocked at what he was doing, running into the middle of the attacking horde, brushing past spiders and zombies, even shoving aside a few endermen, but he didn't care who he provoked or angered. Gameknight had only one thought in mind; save Minecraft.

Reaching the center of the island, Gameknight started to dig straight down, a cardinal sin, a noob kinda thing to do, but he already knew what was underneath this single layer of stone; salvation for all . . . but him. The monsters realized what he was doing and fell on him like a swarm of angry wasps, all of them reaching out to sting him with their jagged claws and sharp teeth. Pain radiated throughout his body as he felt the monsters tear at his flesh. His armor fell away quickly, the iron plating unable to stand up the onslaught, then the real agony began. With claws slashing at him from all around, Gameknight felt as if his nerves were aflame, all of them screaming at him at once, telling him that we would soon be dead, but he didn't care; digging was all the thought about. And so he dug down, quickly punching through the stone block, revealing TNT underneath, an intricate pattern of redstone connecting all of the black and red blocks together.

Dropping his pick, Gameknight pulled out flint and steel and started striking it. He wasn't sure when he'd gotten the fire maker and didn't care. Shooting sparks out, the TNT blocks instantly caught fire, starting to blink, then flame caught to the next and the next. The monsters saw this and stopped their attack. It didn't matter; he was sitting on Minecraft's biggest TNT bomb ever seen. He'd be dead soon, but at least the claws and teeth had stopped tearing at his body. Then the world turned white as the explosion threw him up into the air in a cloud of stone blocks and monster bodies, his own laugh adding to the thunder. Now he understood Crafter, his desire to help others at his own expense. This felt right. More of the TNT detonated in a chain reaction that consumed the entire island, allowing the lava lake to flow in, taking any that survived. As he flew through the air, Gameknight could see Erebus, the endermen flying up to hit the ceiling as more blocks exploded, his eyes glowing with hatred and violence. The dark nightmare then evaporated into a haze of glowing XP particles as his HP quickly extinguishing, the burning white eyes seeming to be the last thing to disappear, still fixed on him. The other monsters also died, their XP adding to the confusion, many of the tiny balls falling into him, his own XP growing exponentially. His laughter continued as he saw the other mobs die, his friends standing at the edge of the cavern, shocked at what they were seeing, disbelief in their eyes.

He'd done it; he's saved this server and all the digital beings that were living their lives here. Finally, he done something completely selfless, and the sense of pride that welled up within him was overwhelming. More XP streamed into him as his life ebbed away. If only he had the chance to continue this, show others that he could be something other than a griefer and a troller . . . if only . . . and then darkness took him as Gameknight999 died.

CHAPTER 17 – Closer to the Source

Gameknight slowly woke, his mind foggy as if reality had somehow merged itself with his fading dream, but what had he been dreaming . . . something about a battle . . . or had that been real . . . He remembered something loud and bright, with creatures floating all around him, each disappearing with a pop leaving behind glowing balls of light, the colorful spheres flowing into him as if pushed by a mighty tornado, the swirling colors followed by calm, sweet darkness. And then he woke here; but where was here?

Looking around, Gameknight saw blocky trees in the distance, their square leaves swaying in the breeze, and cows, lots of cows, each one identical in form and color, their square heads and rectangular bodies fitting in somehow with the terrain.

Minecraft . . . he was still in Minecraft. He sighed. Memories flowed through his mind; the battle with the mobs; Erebus; Shawny and the users; Crafter . . . oh no, Crafter. The image of Crafter's death replayed itself in his head over and over again until he felt a tear start to trickle down his face, his soul filled with an overwhelming sadness. He missed his NPC friend.

Standing, Gameknight999 surveyed the area, trying to push the sadness deep down in his soul. Looking around, he saw that he was amidst low, rolling hills sparsely decorated with oak trees, their mottled bark standing out against the vibrant green grass, the occasional red and yellow flowers adding a dash of extra color to the scene. Yep, he was definitely still in Minecraft; he didn't disconnect. Well, at least he wasn't dead, that has to be on the plus side, but Crafter . . . he dearly missed his friend . . . his smile . . . his humming . . . his joy for life . . .

"Crafter, you didn't die in vain," Gameknight said at the top of his lungs for all to hear, though there was no one in sight, "we won the battle and saved your world."

"Well that's good to know," a high pitched voice said in the distance.

Turning towards the voice, Gameknight saw a young girl, a villager with hands locked across her chest, approaching.

"What?" he asked.

"I said, that's good to know," the young boy replied as he approached.

"What are you talking about?"

"Don't you know who I am?"

"What do you mean?" Gameknight asked. "I've never seen you before."

The boy was short, at least half his height, with long blond hair reaching down to his shoulders. His blocky face was fair in complexion with a gentle smile and a long dark unibrow that spanned his face, standing out in contrast to his dazzling blue eyes. They reminded him of the sky in Minecraft, bright and pure.

"It's me, Crafter," the young villager said, a smile stretching across his face.

"Crafter?"

The young boy nodded.

Gameknight looked at him, confused.

"Here, put your hand on my shoulder," he explained, "and close your eyes. Good. Now reach out with your mind and listen to my voice, not with your ears, but with your entire being, with every part of your body."

Gameknight strained to listen, not sure what he was supposed to do.

A cow mooed in the distance.

"No, relax and listen."

Taking a deep breath and letting it out slowly, he opened all of his senses and listened, really listened, not with his ears, but with his entire being. He could hear the terrain around him, the soil and trees and cows and pigs, all of them ringing with a kind of dissonance that sounded a little like glass scraping against glass to music, harsh and strained tones fighting against each other; it made his teeth hurt. And then the young boy started to hum a soft melody, the harmonious tones filled with peace and tranquility, and a love of life. Crafter . . . he could see Crafter in his mind . . . it was him . . . IT WAS HIM!

"CRAFTER!!!" he yelled, wrapping his arms around his little companion and squeezing tight.

"Easy, easy, I've died once today, I'd rather not do it again."

Gameknight laughed and released his friend.

"You're here . . . but what happened, where is here?"

"We've moved to the next server, closer to the Source," Crafter explained.

It was strange seeing the young boy before him, but seeing his grey-haired companion in his mind.

"But how?"

"All of the XP that I absorbed after detonating the creepers on the bridge allowed me to cross over," Crafter explained. "I suspect something like that must have happened to you as well."

He looked at Gameknight with a questioning look, wanting to hear what had happened.

"Ah . . . well, I detonated the TNT under the island because the redstone was ruined, like on the bridge. I guess all that XP flowed into me as well." Gameknight held out his arms and looked down at them, their blocky shape looking the same as before, but felt somehow different. "I guess I'm still in Minecraft, and didn't get free."

"So you finally did something just to help others, interesting. Maybe you've grown a little, an unexpected outcome," his friend said playfully.

"Yeah, I guess," he replied, a little embarrassed, "but why does this feel so funny, like something's wrong. I can't figure it out, can't describe it other than something is wrong."

"Minecraft is still under attack."

"But I thought we stopped the attack," Gameknight said, confused. "We defeated the mobs and destroyed Erebus."

"That's true," Crafter replied, "but that was only one server. There are many servers leading to this plane, just like there are many on this plane leading to the next. We stopped the invasion on my server, but others must have gotten through. What you're feeling is all the mobs that crossed over and are now attacking this server, trying to get to the Source."

Gameknight closed his eyes and reached out with his mind, feeling for the fabric of Minecraft, the digital mechanism that was working behind the scene, creating everything that he could see, and then he felt it, like a bent gear in a motor or a wheel out of balance. The entire mechanism of Minecraft was off kilter, twisted and disfigured in some indescribable way, but he could feel it as clearly as he could feel the presence of Crafter.

"The battle isn't over," Crafter said, his high pitched voice mixing with the mooing of the nearby cows. "In fact, it's just beginning, and we have to see this through to the end."

"Agreed," Gameknight replied, "but what now?"

"We find a village and start marshaling our forces. I can feel that the battle here will not be fought on the overworld, but somewhere else. It's not quite clear, but we have to get started. We're already behind."

"Then let's go," Gameknight said, patting his friend on the shoulder.

"Pick a direction."

Seeing a rocky mounting just barely visible in the distance, Gameknight chose his direction and started walking, his friend at his side, fear and trepidation nibbling at his soul. The last battle had been bad enough; could they survive this next one? He could still feel the hatred in Erebus as the monster expired, but this world, somehow, seemed to contain much more, so much more. Trying to shake his fear away, he focused on the mountains in the distance. Pulling himself up straight, Gameknight999 and Crafter continued into the unknown, their fate, and the fate of all on this server teetering on the edge of a knife.

The End?

Note from the author:

I hope you enjoyed *Invasion of the Overworld: A Minecraft Novel,* it was fun writing it, but it's more exciting to hear your feedback. Please leave a review at Amazon, Barnes and Noble, Kobo, CreateSpace, Itunes, Smashwords, Diesel, Powell, . . . I would greatly appreciate it, and it will help to accelerate the release of the sequel, coming soon.

Get your Minecraft art into this book!!!

Do you want your Minecraft artwork included in this book. Create a scene in Minecraft that depicts what happens in one of the chapters and take a screen shot, but sure to save it as a jpeg. I'll review all the entries and pick the ones that I think best represent the story and add them in at the beginning of a chapter.

Go to www.markcheverton.com, to the link for this book to upload your images. Be sure to name the image filename with your Minecraft character's name and which chapter you are illustrating. I'll put your name on the image, somewhere, so that everyone will know you made it. There is no guarantee that I'll us an image for all chapters, and there is no guarantee that I'll be able to look at all of them, but I'll do my best. Tell you friends.

Other works by Mark Cheverton

Gameknight999 – Adventures in Minecraft Series
- Invasion of the Overworld: A Minecraft Novel
- Battle for the Nether: The Next Minecraft Novel – *available 2014*
- The End: The Last Minecraft Novel – *Available 2015*

Algae Voices of Azule Series
- Algae Voices of Azule
- Algae Voices of Azule – Book 2: Finding Home
- Algae Voices of Azule – Book 3: Finding the Lost

The Crystal Tear Series
- The Crystal Tear – *Available ???*
- The Faces of the Finder - *Available ???*
- The Breaking of the Krill - *Available ???*

The Algae Voices of Azule

The Algae Voices of Azule is a short story that chronicles a day in the life of a set of twins, Billy and Ali, both ten years old. They are both Gifted, with powers they are just coming to understand. Billy and Ali, however, will be forced to decide if they should use their psychic powers to save someone from a fate worse than death, a choice that may damn them to the same destiny. They'll be hunted by the dreaded Inquisitors, chased through the waterfront and docks of Azule City, and forced to hide for their lives. But when they learned a loved one is in trouble, and only they know how to save them, they will have to make a choice that may damn them forever. Billy and Ali will learn the about the consequences of choice and how cold and terrifying sacrifice can be. You won't be disappointed.

Excerpt from *The Algae Voices of Azule*

"Shhh," Billy answered softly, and then pushed her against the wall of a nearby shop, far into the shadows of first sunrise. Their largest sun, Pateras, had fully risen, the second sun, Gios still hidden behind the curve of Azule allowing them to find these deep, dark shadows, something that was at times a rare commodity when you orbit two suns. "Look, across the street."

Ali shifted her gaze to the street, and gasped. An Inquisitor was walking down the street, dressed in black from head to foot; polished black boots clicking on the concrete pavement, angry black gloves holding a black leather short staff about two feet long, the end wrapped with leather straps that hung loose; his whipping rod as they were called. Around his neck was a thick metal collar, black as night and without any seam. It was almost as if the thing was a part of him; a badge of honor, or horror, that signified him as an Inquisitor. All Gifted slaves wore collars, their color signifying their strength. A few Gifted

156

ever reached the level of brown, and even fewer reached black. Those that did were typically recruited by the Inquisitors or killed, a black Gifted being too much of a threat. This Gifted was clearly well suited to his position. He had an angry, spiteful look on his face, a look that suggested that he just wanted to hurt someone, anyone, he didn't care whom. He was looking for Gifted to capture and put into slavery, a fate worse than death they say. Behind him trailed a squad of military, their lase-guns and plasma rifles held at the ready. The troops walked on both sides of the street, watching the civilians warily, but the Inquisitor chose the center of the street, walking as if he owned it, everyone else as insignificant as the dust underneath his nails. Behind them hover trucks and ground speeders sat waiting, none daring enough to honk their horns and pass through the bristling pincushion of weapons and hate, their anti-gravity generators casting an angry blue glow beneath each floating vehicle.

"Pull in your Gift," Billy said quickly. "Don't let him sense you."

Ali made an angry sound and pulled in her Gift so that she seemed like a shadow of her true self. Inquisitors can sense others using their Gift by stretching out with their own psychic feelings, however, they'd found that it's difficult to sense another Gifted when they pulled in on their Gift, and that was what the twins were doing now, pulling in their psychic energy and hiding it in the deepest, darkest part of their minds.

The Inquisitor looked at their side of the street, and saw the two children standing against the shadowy wall. He took two steps towards them. Billy could feel Ali's fear, hear her starting to cry. They were both terrified. If the Inquisitor came close enough, he'd sense their Gifts, and they'd never see their home or family again. Just as he took another step closer he froze in his tracks and turned his head to the right, looking over his shoulder. Turning around, the Inquisitor pointed into the storefront of a crystal merchant.

"Oh no, Mr. Dirac," Ali whispered to her brother. They'd known for years that he was Gifted. He always kept it to himself, but Ali could tell he was a nice man; this made her sad, and mad.

The squad of soldiers quickly secured the shop and then stormed inside. In no time, they returned dragging a pleading Mr. Dirac out of the shop. The soldiers threw the scared shopkeeper to the ground at the feet of the Inquisitor. He had blood running from his nose and an ugly bruise on the side of his head.

"What do we have here?" the Inquisitor asked with a scratchy voice. "Are you Gifted?"

"Gifted?" Mr. Dirac said in a scared voice. "Me? I'm not one of them, I'm just a crystal merchant, and not a very good one at that. I'm nobody, sir."

"I'm sure the latter is true, but let's see about the former," the Inquisitor croaked. Closing his eyes, he gathered his Gift and extended it into Mr. Dirac's mind. With little compassion or finesse, the Inquisitor probed Dirac's mind, hurting as he searched. The man's moaning made the Inquisitor sick; what a weak excuse for a man, he thought. Probing deeper, Dirac started to scream and crumpled into the fetal position, begging for the pain to stop. It was terrible thing to see, the torture of Mr. Dirac.

Billy could feel the anger start to well up in his sister. Mr. Dirac hadn't done anything wrong, hadn't hurt anyone; he'd just been born the way he was, Gifted. It wasn't a crime, but that's not the way President Macab sees it. Gifted were to be used and then discarded when no longer useful. Ali's anger grew even brighter, leaking outward, her Gift becoming uncontrolled.

"Ali, no," Billy said, pleaded. He pulled her back away, deeper into the shadows, towards a nearby alleyway. "We can't do anything. It's not our problem."

"You sound like Dad," she snapped, the comment intended to hurt her brother; it did.

"We can't save him," he returned, exasperated. "You know the saying, *to be accused by an Inquisitor is to be found guilty.* They're gonna take him, no matter what, now let's get out of here."

Billy turned and started heading down the alley, his hand holding his sister's sweaty hand firmly. He was scared and shaking, and just wanted to get out of there; he didn't want to see what was going to happen on that street, the destruction of a life. As he ran, Ali followed, reluctantly, but he had to pull her, drag her away from the street, from Mr. Dirac. He tried to move faster and pulled on his sister's hand a little harder, but she slipped free causing Billy to trip and fall face first on the ground. At first, the breath was knocked out of him, which elevated his fear, but in a second he was able to take another breath, and then another. His nose was filled with the dust of the alley as he breathed in, trying to understand what had just happened. As he got up, he looked back at his sister. She was standing at the entrance of the alley, feet spread as if expecting a hurricane to take her off her feet, her fists on hips. Billy knew this stance; this was defiance, a refusal to be cowed or intimidated. He'd seen it many times at school, when the bigger kids would pick on them because they were smaller, weaker. Ali would never back down to the bullies, never give an inch, even if it meant being hit or kicked or beat up, she never gave up; he admired her for it, but not now. He could feel the Gift rising up in her, getting ready to lash out at the Inquisitor, lash out at the injustice.

"No, Ali." Billy begged, but he knew it was too late.

Ali's focus was on the Inquisitor and the pain he was inflicting on Mr. Dirac. She didn't really know the crystal merchant, said hi from time to time, but he wasn't a friend, just another person, another Gifted. Gathering her Gift, she formed a ball of air as large as her Gift could muster and began to compress it until it was rock hard. She pulled on her Gift harder than she ever did before, and as she reached the limits of her power, she seemed to feel new areas in her mind open up, with more psychic power there for the asking. Ali drew on all the power she could find, forming the largest, hardest ball of air she could create, and then launched it at the Inquisitor. She then threw more balls of air at the security forces, knocking rifles from hands and tripping up feet.

The ball of air struck the Inquisitor in the shoulder with the force of a battering ram. It knocked him from his feet and stopped the assault of Mr. Dirac's mind. As he fell, his head turned towards Ali and he made eye contact with his attacker.

"A little girl!" the Inquisitor shouted from the street pavement. "I was attacked by a little girl! GET HER!"